THE DARKE
CHRONICLES

THE DARKE CHRONICLES

TALES OF A VICTORIAN PUZZLE–SOLVER

DAVID STUART DAVIES

To friends Barry Forshaw and Peter Guttridge
– two fellows in the know

Illustration: © Chris Senior

First published 2014

The Mystery Press is an imprint of The History Press
The Mill, Brimscombe Port
Stroud, Gloucestershire, GL5 2QG
www.thehistorypress.co.uk

© David Stuart Davies, 2014

British Library Cataloguing in Publication Data.
A catalogue record for this book is available from the British Library.

ISBN 978 0 7524 9770 9

Typesetting and origination by The History Press
Printed in Great Britain

CONTENTS

'Crime is common. Logic is rare. Therefore it is upon logic rather than upon the crime you should dwell.'

Sherlock Holmes in *The Copper Beeches*
by Sir Arthur Conan Doyle

1

THE CURZON STREET CONUNDRUM

Blood was flowing from the wound, forming a neat crimson pool on the carpet. But at least now he was safe. Surely he was safe? And the wound … well, certainly it was serious, but not fatal. He would survive. He tried to reassure himself of this fact as darkness edged in from all corners of his vision, like ink seeping across blotting paper.

Inspector Edward Thornton leaned forward and gazed out of the tiny window of his office in the upper reaches of Scotland Yard. It was a cold November day in 1897 and grey swirls of fog wreathed the adjacent rooftops, reducing them to vague silhouettes. They loomed like giant ghosts, ready to envelop the building.

Thornton sighed wearily at this fancy that so easily took his mind from the very difficult matter in hand. Sergeant Grey looked up from the case notes he was scribbling in his crabbed hand. 'It's not that Curzon Street business is it, sir?'

Thornton replied without moving. 'Of course it is, Grey. There is something not quite right about it, but I cannot fathom out what it is.'

'I don't know what you mean. We've got the blighter who done it safely locked up in the cells. Case solved.'

'Oh, yes, we have someone locked up in the cells, but I'm not so sure it's the "blighter who done it". And if Armstrong really is the murderer, we have so little evidence.'

'There was the blood on his coat.'

'Blood on his coat and the knowledge that he was in great debt to the murdered man. There's not enough material there to weave a hangman's hood, Grey. A good lawyer would blow those flimsy suppositions away in no time. And besides, I need to know how the crime was committed and how the murderer escaped from a locked room.'

Grey dropped his pen on the desk in a gesture of mild irritation. 'Then you know what to do, sir. You know where to go. Don't you? When you've had a real puzzle in the past…'

Thornton turned to his sergeant and pulled his thin, pale face into a mournful grimace. 'Oh, I know all right. I don't need you to tell me. Luther Darke. I have been trying to put off that inevitability for some time.' He stroked his chin in an absent-minded fashion as his eyes flickered with mild irritation. 'There is an element of humiliation in seeking his help. It's an admittance of defeat.'

'Go on, sir. Go and see him. At least it will put your mind at rest.'

Thornton emitted a sigh of resignation and returned his gaze to the grey curtain of fog beyond the windows.

Luther Darke poured himself a large whisky and sat back in his chair. As he did so, a lithe black cat leapt onto his lap with practised ease, curled up tightly, and began to purr. Absent-mindedly, he stroked the contented creature as he stared across at his visitor, his dark brown eyes shining. He raised his glass in a mock toast. 'It is good to see you again, Edward. I am sorry that you will not join me in a drink. However, I am sure it is a wise move. Respectable gentlemen should not drink before noon, and then decorum decrees that it should be a sherry aperitif.' He took a gulp of whisky, rolling it around his mouth. 'Whisky is the milk of the Gods; sherry is their urine.'

Thornton remained silent. Like an actor waiting for his cue, he knew when it would be his time to speak. This preamble was a variant of the usual extravagant felicitations that he always experienced when he visited Luther Darke.

'To be honest, Edward, I am surprised to see you under my roof once more,' said his host, affably. 'You disagreed with me so strongly in the Baranokov affair – until my theory was proved correct that triplets had been used as a ploy in the theft of diamonds – that I thought I had lost your friendship for ever.'

Thornton blushed slightly; partly for being reminded of his failure in the Baranokov case, and partly because this strange man referred to him as a friend. He didn't think anyone could get close enough to Darke to become his friend. He was too enigmatic, too self-possessed, too complicated to give himself to straightforward friendship. There was Carla, of course, his lover, but she in her own way was just as mysterious and enigmatic as Darke himself.

Luther Darke was the son of a duke but, because of his undisciplined and outrageous behaviour, he had become estranged from his widowed father at an early age. He had been a rebel and hated the arrogance and pomposity of the aristocracy. Although Darke had inherited a considerable amount of money on his father's death, he had passed over the title and the family home to his younger brother, of whom he saw little. Ducal respectability and responsibility were abhorrent to him. He now occupied most of his time in being an artist – a portrait painter – and was gaining a growing reputation for his work. But even here, his energies were erratic. On a whim he would drop his brush halfway through a painting in order to follow up one of his other passions, which were very varied and eclectic. He had a fascination for the unexplained and the unknown. He took a great interest in the work of spiritualist mediums and unsolved crimes. It was his offer of assistance in the Carmichael mystery, when Foreign Office official Ralph Carmichael, his wife and two children – along with their pet spaniel – apparently disappeared into thin air that had brought

Inspector Thornton into contact with this unique individual for the first time. Darke helped to solve the case and Thornton had sought his assistance several times since. However, after the Baranokov affair, over which they had disagreed violently, there had been a rift in their relationship. Thornton was well aware that it was he who, suffering from the humiliation of being proved wrong, had turned his back on his strange associate. But here he was again, seeking Darke's assistance and hoping earnestly that it would be offered.

Luther Darke took another gulp of whisky. 'Ah, we see the world from different hilltops, you and I, Edward. You are the professional, scientific detective with a demand for rationality and feasibility; whereas I am the amateur, an artist, doomed to view things from a different angle and able to see shifting and often unusual perspectives. We are two halves of the perfect whole.' He grinned at his own conceit and his eyes glittered mischievously. He had a broad, mobile saturnine face that possessed a wide, fleshy mouth. Dark, expressive eyebrows topped a pair of soft brown eyes that radiated warmth. His head was framed by a mane of luxurious hazel-coloured hair. He would have been handsome, but the crooked nose, broken in one of the many fights he had at school, robbed him of the classical symmetry of male beauty. He was not handsome then, but he had a magnetic presence that compelled one to watch his face with fascination as Thornton did. Every conversation was a performance. It was as though he was acting out his life.

'So, enough teasing. The Curzon Street murder? Am I right?'

Thornton nodded. 'I am not happy about it.'

'From what I have read in the papers, the case seems a straightforward one.' Darke placed his whisky glass on the table by his chair and steepled his fingers. 'Let me see. Shipping magnate Laurence Wilberforce is murdered at his Curzon Street mansion – stabbed – and one of the guests in his house at the time was a certain Richard Armstrong, who owed the magnate a considerable amount of money that he could not repay. To make matters worse, I believe that blood was found smeared on the wretched fellow's overcoat. Have I caught the essence of the matter?'

Thornton gave a thin smile. 'You knew I'd come to you.'

Darke's eyes twinkled with humour. 'Indeed, I did. I was sure my worthy Thornton would not be taken in by such a simplistic solution. No doubt your superiors are quite content with Armstrong's arrest and cannot wait to see him dangling at the end of a rope.'

'They are indeed, despite the fact that one essential element of the case still remains a mystery.'

'And that is?'

'How the murder was committed.'

Darke laughed. 'Just a minor irritation. Not worth considering, surely? Pull the lever and let's have done with the scoundrel.'

Thornton's sensitive face darkened. There was more truth in Darke's flippant observations than was comfortable.

'I presume that Armstrong has not confessed in some fit of madness?'

'On the contrary, he professes his innocence most strongly.'

Darke beamed, his face alive with excitement. 'So, young friend, we have come to that precious, that essential moment: give me the facts. Give me the minutiae.'

Thornton nodded. 'Do you mind if I walk about while I talk? It will help me recall the details more clearly.'

'The house is yours.'

'This room will do.'

'That's one of the things I like about you, Edward. You are so literal. Pray begin.'

'The murder occurred three nights ago at the Curzon Street mansion of Laurence Wilberforce. There was a small dinner party with six guests, business associates of Wilberforce, some of whom brought their wives.'

'Armstrong's wife was there?'

'He's a widower.'

'Ah. Another avenue closed. Resume.'

'There were Lord and Lady Clarendon; Mr Clive Brownlow, the Member of Parliament for Slough and his wife, Sarah; Jack Stavely, a junior partner in one of Wilberforce's concerns and apparently very much a blue-eyed boy. And Armstrong.'

'And Armstrong.'

'Richard Armstrong who until recently worked for Wilberforce as a designer but left twelve months ago to set up his own business, helped by a generous loan from his old boss. But part of the arrangement was that he had to pay the money back within the year.'

'How much?'

'£5,000.'

Darke pursed his lips. 'A considerable sum.'

'One which he could not repay.'

'You know this for certain?'

'Indeed. He freely admits it. His business is in great financial difficulties. Only the previous week he had written to Wilberforce asking for more time to settle the debt.'

'And the old boy refused?'

Thornton nodded. 'Apparently Wilberforce was a harsh, unsentimental man in business.'

'And that is seen as a motive for murder.'

Thornton nodded.

'Very well. So what happened?'

'All the guests had arrived, but Wilberforce had not shown his face. Mrs Wilberforce, Beatrice, was somewhat annoyed at his non-appearance. Apparently, he had retired upstairs to his dressing room over an hour before and had not been seen since. She sent up their butler, a fellow called Boldwood, to inform him that the guests had arrived. The butler returned some minutes later to say that Wilberforce was not in his dressing room, but that the door to his study, a chamber that adjoined the dressing room, was locked and a light could been seen at the bottom of the door. Somewhat concerned, Mrs Wilberforce asked Jack Stavely to go upstairs with her to investigate. It was as the butler had said. The study door was not only locked, but it was bolted – and bolted from the inside, thus clearly indicating that there was someone within. After knocking on the door for some moments to no avail, it was felt that perhaps Wilberforce had fallen ill and was in no fit state to withdraw the bolt. With Mrs Wilberforce's permission, Jack Stavely broke the door down. And what a tragic sight met their eyes.'

'Describe this tragic sight.'

'Lying on the floor in a pool of his own blood was the master of the house. Near to his body was a long-bladed knife. The man was dead.'

Darke rubbed his hands with glee. 'Fascinating. One assumes he died as a result of being stabbed.'

'There was just one knife wound to the stomach.'

'A pretty puzzle, Edward. How could the murderer leave the room if it was bolted on the inside?'

'Precisely.'

'There is no suggestion that this was an elaborate suicide?'

The policeman shook his head. 'Practically it is possible, I suppose, but it would take tremendous courage to stab oneself in the stomach in such a way. However, I am certain that it was not suicide. There was no reason for him to take his life. Life was very good for Laurence Wilberforce. I've checked both his medical records and his financial situation. He was very healthy in both departments. And besides, suicide was just not Wilberforce's way.'

'Well, let's hear the end of this captivating tale.'

'The Yard was summoned and I was assigned to the case. Before I arrived, Jack Stavely discovered one of the visitors' coats smeared with fresh blood. It was still damp. It turned out that the coat belonged to Richard Armstrong. Stavely immediately accused Armstrong of the murder. Sergeant Grey had to restrain him from attacking Armstrong. Mrs Wilberforce then showed us a letter her husband had received from Armstrong, in which veiled threats were made to Wilberforce. He said he needed more time to pay his debts, adding something like … 'if you are intent on breaking me on the wheel in this matter, the consequences will be far the worse for you.'

'Nicely phrased. So on these two pieces of evidence – a smear of blood and an angry letter – you arrested Armstrong for the murder of Laurence Wilberforce.'

'I had no alternative. Sometimes one has to do things one doesn't believe in, especially as a public servant. But the more I've considered the matter, the less convinced I am that Armstrong is the guilty party. But I don't know why. I think the key to the whole problem is how the murder was committed.'

'Indeed. My very thought, too. Let us go back to this study for a moment. Describe it to me.'

'It is a small room, some ten feet square. There was a fireplace, with a fire burning in the grate. The chimney aperture was too narrow to allow access.'

'Even for a child?'

Thornton gaped. He hadn't thought of that. 'Even a child,' he said at length.

'Window?'

'There was no window and no ceiling trap. We've had the carpet up and moved the desk and bookcase, which were the only pieces of furniture placed against a wall.'

'So in essence what we have is a sealed box with a door.'

'Yes. And that was bolted from the inside.'

'A very pretty puzzle indeed, Inspector Thornton. I thank you for bringing it to my notice.'

'But can you solve it?'

'Oh, yes.' Darke gave his companion a lazy grin. 'All one needs to do is to view the problem from a different angle.' With great care he lifted the sleeping cat from his lap and placed it down on the rug before the fire. It stirred fitfully in its slumbers and then, shifting its position slightly, returned to its feline dreams. 'Sorry, Persephone, my friend,' he murmured gently, 'but I have to leave you now.' Swilling the remainder of his whisky down, he turned to his visitor with enthusiasm. 'What say you, Edward? I think it best if we visit the scene of crime together; then we can really get to grips with this mystery.'

The two men decided to walk from Darke's town house in Manchester Square to Curzon Street. 'The sharp autumnal air will revitalise the brain cells,' Darke observed as George, his manservant, helped him on with his overcoat.

Although it was only just after noon, the November day was already darkening, and the fog that earlier had begun to disperse was now thickening and closing in once more, cloaking the city in a bleary haze. Their fellow pedestrians loomed as dark silhouetted phantoms before them. It was the sort of weather that Darke liked, and he felt at home in its sooty embrace.

'Tell me about Wilberforce's wife, Beatrice,' he said, as Thornton fell into step with him. 'Was she very upset when she found her husband?'

'Naturally, she was distressed.'

'But this distress quickly turned to anger.'

'What do you mean?'

'Well, when the blood was discovered on Armstrong's coat, you said she very promptly produced the letter with the well-phrased threat, determined to prove that he was the culprit. Her husband's murderer.'

'Yes.'

'So the lady was able to repress her grief sufficiently to retrieve this missive, one which strengthens the guilt of Armstrong. All which suggests that anger, rather than grief, was governing her actions. What do you know of their marriage?'

'There was very little gossip about it. They have been married for twenty-two years and have no children. It was rumoured that in the early days Laurence Wilberforce was something of a ladies' man, but...'

'Age cools the ardour, eh? I met the man once. A cold fish, as I recall. There was no humour or *joie de vivre* in his demeanour.'

'A business man.'

Darke laughed heartily. 'Precisely – you put your finger on it, Edward. The concerns of profit and loss place a handcuff on your soul.'

'Do you suspect Mrs Wilberforce of the murder?'

'No more than Armstrong, I suppose,' said Darke. 'In one sense she is the natural beneficiary: she loses a humourless husband and inherits his wealth. Motives enough, you will agree.'

Edward Thornton fell silent. An image of Beatrice Wilberforce flashed into his mind. A small, slender woman in her late forties, with her blonde hair turning grey. Her pale, rather pinched face had once been girlishly pretty but now it was set ready, eager almost, for old age. Did she have the determination and malevolence to carry out the cold-blooded murder of her husband and then implicate Armstrong? Well, even if she did, how did she do it? That problem remained.

Thornton's reverie was broken by Darke's announcement: 'Well, my boy, it seems that we have arrived at our destination.'

Sure enough, the two men stood before the Wilberforce mansion in Curzon Street. The lights from the windows shimmered through the moist net of the fog.

'Lay on, Macduff,' cried Darke, pushing the inspector towards the door.

The butler, Boldwood, received the visitors and invited them to wait in the hall while he informed his mistress of their presence. He was a tall, dignified man, prematurely bald, with a naturally reserved and melancholic manner. As he walked away in a stiff, erect fashion, Darke nudged his companion. 'By the look of his gait, our friend Boldwood was recruited from the ranks – an ex-soldier, sergeant probably – and that scar on his neck suggests that he has seen some action.'

'Is that relevant to the case?'

Darke grinned and shrugged his shoulders in a nonchalant fashion.

Within minutes, Boldwood returned. 'Mrs Wilberforce will see you in the drawing room, but I beg you gentlemen to keep your visit as short as possible. My mistress has not yet recovered her strength after her terrible loss.' Although couched in formal terms, the statement was more of an order than a request.

'We shall be a brief as possible,' said Thornton.

'Served in India, did we, Boldwood?' asked Luther Darke.

The butler eyed his interrogator with suspicion. 'I did, sir. 101st Bengal Fusiliers.'

'Good man. The rank of sergeant, I should guess.'

'Yes, sir.'

Boldwood paused for a moment, staring intently into Darke's face with some puzzlement, and then neatly turning on his heel, he led them to the drawing room. As he held the door open, Darke leaned over and addressed him again. 'I think it would be propitious if you join us, Boldwood, old boy. You can help fill in certain pieces of the puzzle.'

Reluctantly the tall manservant entered the room and positioned himself by the door.

Beatrice Wilberforce rose from the chaise longue on which she had been reclining to greet her visitors. Her face was gaunt and dark circles ringed her pale blue eyes. She seemed not to notice Boldwood's presence. She looked with some disdain at her two visitors.

'What can I do for you, Inspector?' Her voice was weary and distant.

Before Thornton could respond to this request, Darke moved forward and gave a low theatrical bow. 'I am the one you can assist, dear lady. Luther Darke, a seeker of truth.'

The woman seemed somewhat taken aback by this effusive stranger in her drawing room and involuntarily she sat down on the chaise longue as if she needed it for support.

'Mr Darke is assisting me in my enquiries,' ventured Thornton for clarification.

Mrs Wilberforce's sour expression remained intact.

Darke moved closer to her and addressed her in the softest of tones. 'I wonder if I can prevail upon you to recount the events on the evening of your husband's passing,' he said.

Beatrice Wilberforce glanced over at Thornton. 'But I have already told the inspector everything I know several times.'

'But you have not told me.'

A flicker of irritation passed across her brow, but it was gone in an instant. 'If … if you think it will help.'

'It may save a man's life.'

Mrs Wilberforce seemed puzzled, but she made no comment on Darke's enigmatic claim. In a firm, clear voice, she began to recount the events of the evening when her husband had died. 'We were having a little dinner party – for no special reason. It was just a social occasion.'

'Who drew up the guest list?'

'I did … in consultation with my husband, of course.'

'Of course. What was the purpose of inviting Richard Armstrong to this soirée? There was bad blood between him and Mr Wilberforce, was there not?'

'It was my idea. The bad blood you refer to was purely a business matter and not personal on my husband's side. Business was one thing; friendship another. Laurence was a strict man of business and he expected – and indeed demanded – others to be so. Sometimes this led him to act in what I suppose was regarded by some as an unreasonable manner – but he could be reasoned with. I thought that in a relaxed, informal atmosphere, some amicable arrangement between Armstrong…' Her eyes misted and she clutched the edge of the chaise. Her lips tightened as she fought to control her feelings and it struck Darke that she was dismayed at betraying her own emotions. It seemed to him that she saw this as a great weakness. It wasn't the memory of her husband or the events of that fateful evening that distressed Beatrice Wilberforce, but the cracks in her own reserve. 'As it turned out,' she said at length, 'inviting that man to dinner was the worst decision I could have made.'

She reached for a handkerchief, but there was none. Darke flashed the cream silk one from his jacket breast pocket and pressed it into her hand. As he did so, his eyes were caught by a mark on the woman's arm.

'At what time did you last see your husband alive?'

'At around six o'clock,' Mrs Wilberforce replied, dabbing her eyes with the handkerchief. 'He said he was going to his study to write some letters and then have a long soak in the bath before the party.'

'Were any letters found?' This question Darke addressed to Thornton. The policeman shook his head.

'Who laid out his evening clothes?'

'Boldwood, of course.'

Darke turned to the butler with a quizzical glance.

'That's right, sir.'

'Did you see your master while you attended to this task?'

'No, sir. The study door was closed.'

Darke shut his eyes for a moment and sighed heavily. He raised his hand slightly as if he were reaching out for something. The room fell silent as the others waited for him to return to them. At length his eyes sprang open and, with a ghost of a smile playing about his lips, he resumed his questioning of Mrs Wilberforce. 'Who were the first guests to arrive?'

'I ... I can't really say for sure, everyone came more or less at the same time. I think Lord and Lady Clarendon were the first.' She grinned briefly. 'I know Jack Stavely was last – and late.' Her grin broadened. 'He's always late.'

'He comes here a great deal?'

Beatrice Wilberforce nodded, her face resuming its pained expression. 'He is a regular visitor.'

'You were cross when your husband did not appear to greet his guests.'

'Yes. I felt sure he had become absorbed with his correspondence and lost track of the time. I asked Boldwood to check on him for me.'

With a wave of the hand, Darke indicated that Boldwood should come closer and join the inner circle. 'Tell me, Sergeant Boldwood, what happened next?'

'I went up to Mr Wilberforce's dressing room. He wasn't there and neither were his evening clothes, so I assumed that he had bathed and dressed and was now in his study. I tapped on the door. There was no reply. I tapped again, louder this time in case he had nodded off, and informed him that the guests for the party had arrived. There was still no reply. Then I tried the door. It was locked.'

'Did he often lock it?'

'Never when he was inside the room.'

'What did you do next?'

'I went downstairs to inform Mrs Wilberforce.'

'Were you worried?'

'I … I thought that it was strange.'

'And then with Mrs Wilberforce and Jack Stavely, you returned to the room and Stavely broke down the study door.'

Boldwood nodded and bowed his head.

'The door was bolted on the inside, Mrs Wilberforce. Is that correct?'

Suddenly the widow's patience snapped and Darke witnessed the flame of anger that burned inside that soft and timid exterior. 'You know it is! How long is this tirade of questions going on? Why must you put me under this torture yet again? I cannot tell you any more than I have already told you. My husband is dead and all you can do is make me relive that dreadful evening when he died. Have you no tact or manners?'

'Gentlemen, I think it best if you leave,' said Boldwood, taking a pace forward. There was more than a hint of aggression in his demeanour.

Darke grinned back at the butler. 'Distressed though your mistress is, Sergeant Boldwood, I am sure that she is also very concerned that the person who killed her husband is caught and tried for his murder. She would not want to hinder the course of justice.'

'But the police have caught him,' snapped Mrs Wilberforce, the anger still vibrant in her voice. 'Richard Armstrong. Inspector Thornton arrested him.'

'An arrest doth not a conviction make. You seem so very certain that he was your husband's murderer.'

Boldwood took another step nearer to Darke, his eyes blazing, but Beatrice Wilberforce stopped him in his tracks with a spirited glance.

'In order to allow you to recover your equilibrium, Mrs Wilberforce,' said Luther Darke smoothly, 'perhaps you will allow Boldwood to show us your husband's dressing room and study so that we may examine the scene of the crime?'

'Yes.' Her reply was hardy audible. 'As you wish.'

As Boldwood led the two men upstairs, Thornton held his companion back a few steps and whispered in his ear. 'You were rather harsh on the poor woman,' he hissed.

Darke nodded. 'I overstepped the bounds of decency – again. I shall repent. Boldwood, old fellow, pause a moment, will you? I just want to apologise for my brutish behaviour towards your mistress. It was unforgivable.'

The butler turned to face Darke; his face was stern. 'I must confess, sir, if it had not been for the thought of disturbing Mrs Wilberforce further, I should have struck you for your insolence.'

'And I should have deserved it. The lady is lucky in having such a chivalrous protector. You have been with her long?'

'Five years.'

'Mr Wilberforce was a good employer?'

'He … he was, sir.'

'They were a happy couple? The marriage was a sound one?'

Boldwood's face blanched with anger. 'How dare you! That is none of your damned business. What right have you to come here…?'

Darke halted this sudden outburst by holding up his hands in a mock surrender. 'There I go again, overstepping the mark. I shall say no more. Pray continue.'

Without a word, the butler carried on up the stairs. Thornton and Darke followed, with the latter giving his companion a huge wink.

At length the two men were shown into the dressing room of the murdered man.

'You can leave us now, Boldwood. Inspector Thornton and I need to inspect these rooms alone. We shall not be too long.'

The butler hesitated by the door.

Thornton gave a polite cough to initiate the servant's departure. 'Thank you, Boldwood. We shall make our own way downstairs.'

With reluctance, Boldwood left the room.

'Now,' said Darke, rubbing his hands, 'show me this magic study.'

Thornton led him to the rear of the dressing room and flung open the study door to reveal a small, dark chamber beyond containing a desk, a chair and a small bookcase. There was a fireplace on the far wall. Thornton switched on the electric light, which bathed the study in a suffuse amber glow.

As soon as Darke had entered the room, he examined the door. 'Was the key found to the study?'

'No,' said Thornton kneeling beside him. 'But it was bolted, too, remember.'

'Oh, indeed, I do remember. This is the poor thing hanging off here.'

'It was damaged when Jack Stavely broke down the door.'

'Mm. He did us something of a favour. Look here, Thornton, at these screws: they are new and the bolt is shiny and unmarked.' He indicated where the bolt had been attached to the door. 'Notice the portion of wood which had been covered by the bolt before Mr Stavely's boot came into play. It is the same colour as the surrounding wood. There is no differentiation whatsoever.'

'What are you saying?'

'That this bolt is new, very new. It cannot have been there for very long. If it had been in place for any length of time, the wood beneath it would be of a different hue. See the screw holes, how white and fresh the wood is. And, my friend, most damning of all…'

Darke scooped up a few white specks from the carpet. 'Sawdust,' he explained. 'From the screw holes. It is possible that the bolt was only fixed there on the day of the murder.'

'This is all very well, but I fail to see how this throws any fresh light on the identity of the killer, or indeed on the way in which the murder was committed.'

'Patience, my friend.'

Darke had now moved to the centre of the room and was examining a dark stain on the carpet. 'Wilberforce's blood, I suppose?'

'Yes.'

'Not as large a pool as I had expected, but that fits the theory which is forming nicely in my mind. I suppose the knife is at Scotland Yard.'

'It is.'

'Describe it to me.'

'It's a long-handled knife. Dull metal with some simple carvings and a longish blade which curves slightly at the end.'

Darke sat at the desk and sketched out a crude drawing. 'Something like that?'

'Why, yes...' Before Thornton could say more, a strident voice called out: 'What the Devil is going on here?' Both men turned to discover a young man standing in the doorway of the study. He was short of stature and had his hands on his hips in an aggressive manner.

'Mr Stavely,' said Thornton.

'Yes, Inspector, and you will answer to your superiors for this – barging into Mrs Wilberforce's house and upsetting the lady.'

'News travels fast, eh, Edward?' observed Darke with a flicker of amusement.

'You may do what you wish, Mr Stavely,' said Thornton, approaching the intruder so that he towered over him comfortably. 'But there is no case of "barging" anywhere. We were invited into the house, and as a police officer I am carrying out my duties in a murder enquiry. I would hope you have no wish to hinder that enquiry.'

Stavely hesitated. 'But the enquiry is closed. You have the wretch who murdered Laurence.'

Darke joined his friend and placed a hand on his shoulder. 'It is amazing how everyone is so certain that an innocent man who had the misfortune to owe Wilberforce a lot of money is guilty of his murder.'

'And who the hell are you?'

'I, sir, am Abraham attempting to drink from the well of truth. And how did you learn of our visit?'

'I have just arrived. I have called every day since the murder to spend some time with Beatrice, Mrs Wilberforce.'

'And Boldwood informed you of my dreadful behaviour.'

'Yes.'

'Well, sir, I have apologised to him and I will apologise to you. Any rudeness on my part was calculated in order to bring this mysterious case to a swift conclusion. I am afraid Boldwood may have been more concerned about what we may find in here rather than our apparent disrespectful ways. I suspect he was hoping that your heroic intervention would put a stop to our scrutiny of this chamber.'

Stavely's face clouded with confusion. 'What on earth do you mean?'

'Mr Stavely, let us do a deal together. I will tell you some of the matter, on the proviso that you help us with a little subterfuge. Is that agreed?'

It was just over thirty minutes later that Thornton and Darke sat in the drawing room with Beatrice Wilberforce and Jack Stavely. Boldwood had just served tea and was about to leave the room when Thornton stopped him. 'You had better remain,' he said. 'What Mr Darke has to say will be of great interest to you.'

'Come, sit down, man,' cried Darke, indicating a seat next to Stavely.

Casting an apprehensive glance at his mistress, he pulled up a chair.

'Now, Mr Darke, you have been mysterious, you have been rude and you have been persuasive. Pray tell us what this is all about,' said Beatrice Wilberforce.

Luther Darke placed his cup and saucer on the tea trolley and stood facing the small group. 'Murder most foul, as in the best it is. Inspector Thornton here sought my assistance because he was far from convinced that the poor devil languishing in the cells at Scotland Yard was the perpetrator of the crime that was committed here a few evenings ago. After hearing the details of the case, I was certain that debtor Armstrong was innocent. It was all too convenient. Anyone capable of carrying out a clever murder in a locked room would not have been careless enough to leave some blood on his outdoor coat. It was a foolish embellishment, placed there in order to establish a scapegoat. I had my own ideas concerning the method of the murder, but I needed to discover a few further details before I could be certain. Now I am certain.' He retrieved his cup and drank some tea as his audience absorbed this information. It was a brave act on his part. He abhorred tea, and as a rule it never passed his lips.

'In the detection of crime, sixth sense and guesswork play a valid part in reaching the right conclusion. On very slender evidence, I guessed or at least sensed that the marriage between Laurence and Beatrice Wilberforce was not a completely happy one.' He raised his hand to silence Mrs Wilberforce before she could protest.

'I do not wish to speak ill of the dead, but Laurence Wilberforce was a humourless, cold-hearted bully who could turn nasty even towards someone of whom he once thought kindly. His treatment of Richard Armstrong bears witness of that. As does the bruising on your arm. You have been badly used, my dear.'

The woman said nothing, but stared determinedly ahead of her, avoiding Darke's gaze.

'The bruising gave some foundation to my surmise. Similarly, Boldwood's angry reticence when I questioned him concerning the state of the Wilberforce marriage added more grist to my mill. Boldwood revealed himself as a great protector of his mistress. What did you say, Sergeant? Something like: "I would have knocked you down for being so impertinent but it would have upset

Mrs Wilberforce." Words to that effect. A real Sir Galahad. How difficult it must have been for you, Boldwood, to live and serve in a house where the husband treated his wife miserably and on occasion, struck her with some violence. Hard for a man who loved his mistress and wanted to protect her. Here you were, an old military man used to action, used to fighting for what you believed in, but unable to do anything about the injustice going on under your nose. But, oh, there are straws – there are straws, apparently insignificant, puny little straws, which yet have, as the proverb has it, the power to break a camel's back.

'On the day of the murder, Wilberforce was in a foul mood. Probably he had seen the guest list and noticed Armstrong's name. He lost his temper and behaved abominably. The bruises that are now fading from his wife's arm were, I am sure, administered on that day. For you Boldwood, late of the 101st Bengal Fusiliers, this was your last straw. You conceived a plan to rid your mistress of this troublesome husband. It was a well-wrought plan indeed.'

Boldwood made to rise, but Thornton, who had manoeuvred his way around the back of the butler's chair, placed both hands on his shoulders and gently pressed him back into his seat.

'I cannot be sure how accurate I am as to the minutiae but I am sure that my broad strokes paint the true picture. Boldwood bought a bolt from the local ironmongers. We found the bag in which it was wrapped and the receipt stuffed in the drawer in his room. I am sorry, Boldwood, but with Mr Stavely's connivance we searched your room just now, while he busied you with other chores. Like many murderers before you, you were confident that you would never be suspected or that your room would be searched. We also discovered the screwdriver you used to fix the bolt on the inside of Wilberforce's study. Then you waited. Waited until your master had dressed for dinner, before you entered his dressing room armed with a knife. You told him, no doubt, what a despicable creature he was. How he was a monster ruining the life of one of the finest women you had known. And he, no doubt, laughed at first…'

'He did laugh. Until he saw the knife.' Boldwood uttered these words in monotone, without a trace of emotion showing on his face. 'And then the coward stopped laughing.'

'You stabbed him once. That was all that was necessary. And then with the knife still lodged in his stomach, you pushed him into the study. You stood outside the room, uttering curses and threats about how you intended to finish him off. In desperation, he attempted to shut the door on you, and you let him. One can but imagine his surprise and delight to find that the door now possessed a bolt. His disordered brain would not question how it got there. For Wilberforce it was a Godsend. His desperate hands slammed it home, thus trapping himself within his own tomb.'

Boldwood said nothing, but a fevered light illuminated his eyes as, through Darke's narrative, he relived the moment.

Darke continued: 'Although badly wounded, Laurence Wilberforce now thought that he was safe. What he didn't know – what no one knew or suspected – was that the tip of the knife had been tainted with a strong poison which brought about death within five minutes or so. The stain on the carpet suggested to me that Wilberforce's blood loss was not that great as to bring about his death with such alacrity. He had to be helped on his way. A blade tipped with poison was the most obvious device. No doubt the deadly concoction was one of the prizes that you brought back with you from India, along with the knife. I know of few soldiers who served out there who did not bring back one of those long-handled knives as a rather gruesome reminder of their Indian sojourn. The bazaars were full of them. "A souvenir, sahib?"'

'Is this all true, Boldwood?' asked Beatrice Wilberforce, her voice no louder than a harsh whisper.

'It is all true,' came the solemn reply.

The woman rose to her feet, her face suddenly flushed with anger. 'You fool, you damned fool!' she screamed. 'Don't you know that whatever Laurence did to me, I loved him? I loved him with all my heart. He was my husband! And now you have taken him away.'

She made a mad dash for the servant, but Jack Stavely stepped forward and held her back. She sank into his arms, sobbing.

Boldwood looked in horror at his mistress. His features blanched at the sudden realisation that he had been both blind and foolish. He turned sharply, as if to make for the door.

'Don't bother with that, Boldwood. You will find there are two constables and my assistant Sergeant Grey waiting outside, ready to take you to the Yard,' said Edward Thornton, stepping forward and clasping a pair of handcuffs on the man. He had visibly shrunk, and his eyes moistened with tears. 'I did it for the best, sir. I did it for m'lady.'

At this reference to her Beatrice Wilberforce pulled away from Jack Stavely. 'Get out of my sight, you devil. I never want to see you again.'

Luther Darke poured himself another large whisky. Thornton clapped his hands over his glass. One large nip was enough for him, but not for his triumphant friend.

'I need this as an antidote to that tea with which I sullied my throat in Curzon Street,' he said with solemnity.

The two men were seated around the fire in Darke's sitting room later that day. Persephone still lay like a wax image, curled in a foetal position, before the grate.

Darke took a gulp from his glass and rolled the liquid around in his mouth before swallowing it slowly, allowing its warmth to burn his throat. He grinned. '"Gie me ae spark 'o Nature's fire, That's a' learning I desire," as Maester Burns has it. Well, Edward, a successful day: the solving of a murder and the release of an innocent man.'

'Indeed, but it gave me no pleasure to lock up Boldwood. He is a sad creature whose intentions were for the best.'

'Misplaced affection, passion as it was in Boldwood's case, can drive a man to behave like the Devil. And it was a devilishly ingenious plan. He knew with the evidence of a stab wound, the pool of blood and the knife, that no one would think of poison as the real cause of death. The locked room was also an added subterfuge to fog the truth. A real November crime, eh? Remember, he was virtually making the rules of his murder plan up as he went along. He was determined to muddy the waters as much as possible. If Boldwood had not tried to be too clever by smearing Armstrong's coat with blood, he might even have got away with it.'

'Because then there would have been no definite suspect and nothing to prompt my unease which sent me running to you.'

'I cannot believe that you came running. With a dignified policeman-like gait, surely.'

Thornton laughed. The whisky was already going to his head. 'I had better be on my way. There is work still to be done back at the Yard.'

Luther Darke saw Edward Thornton to the door. Thick winter night, with its grey coils of fog, awaited the inspector beyond the threshold.

'Thank you for your help, Luther. You are an amazing man.'

For a moment, Darke's face grew serious. 'We are all amazing men in our own way, my friend. Come again soon.'

With that, the two men shook hands and Thornton walked out into the darkness, which soon swallowed him up. Darke returned to his fireside, his cat and his whisky.

2

THE PUZZLE OF THE INNOCENT MURDERER

There was a gleam in the eye, one of great pleasure and satisfaction, as the knife came down. It came down again, and again and again. Out of such destruction, thought the wielder of the knife, we create a new kind of justice.

Luther Darke propped himself up in bed, his head resting on a large white pillow, and gazed across the room at the naked form of his mistress, Carla, as she sat with her back to him by the dressing table, combing her dark tresses. 'Come back to bed and hold me once more,' he murmured in a mock romantic voice.

Carla giggled. 'You may have all the time in the world to make love in the afternoon, my fine fellow, but I have a train to catch.'

Darke groaned loudly. This time there was no humour in his response. 'Must you go?'

'I must, and you know I must. I explained all this to you before you lured me into your bed.'

'Lured! I take exception to the word "lured", madam,' he said laughing, plucking at an imaginary moustache. ''Twas a mutual contract, I warrant.'

Carla's red lips parted in a broad smile. She crossed to the bed, knelt by Darke and gave him a long sensuous kiss. 'And it was mutually enjoyed, I can assure the gentleman. But now I must go. I shall only be away a few days. I am sure that he can be patient until I return.'

'Impatient and pining. But be off with you, you strumpet, I do not wish to incur your mother's wrath by causing you to miss the train.'

'That's better.' Carla jumped up and began to get dressed.

Darke watched her with great affection. With an artist's eye as well as that of a lover, he observed the delicate and graceful figure before him as she dressed herself. And then the main cause of his unhappiness connected with her imminent departure flashed into his brain. 'But how am I going to survive Lord Neville's party tomorrow night? You know how I hate these ghastly affairs. It is only the fact that the most beautiful and intelligent woman in London accompanies me to such functions that makes them the least bit tolerable.'

'Don't go. Feign illness and send a note of excuse.'

'I can hardly do that, my sweet. I am the guest of honour after all. Have you forgotten that Neville is unveiling my portrait of him at this blasted soirée?'

'No, of course I haven't,' Carla replied, smoothing down her dress. 'Oh, don't look so petulant, Luther. You resemble a rather miserable little schoolboy who has been give double Latin homework.'

Darke laughed. 'I feel like a miserable little schoolboy.'

'Now, Luther, you know I can't go with you, so why not take someone else?'

'Who?'

'What about that policeman friend of yours?'

'Thornton? Why him?'

'Unlike you, I'm sure he would find the occasion interesting and exciting – amusing, even.'

Pursing his lips, Darke considered the suggestion. 'Mmm, it is an idea. I like Edward. He's good, intelligent company, which is more than can be said for Lord Neville.'

'There you are then. Take him along and you'll hardly miss me at all.'

'Ah, Carla, I would miss my heart less than I would miss you.' His voice had lost its playful tone and the genuine sentiment crackled in the silence it created. Their eyes met, but they said nothing.

'It is my brother's dress suit,' said Inspector Edward Thornton the following evening as he slipped off his overcoat by Darke's fireside.

Darke scrutinised the outfit. 'Quite respectable, if a little historical. Now, a snifter before we venture into the night and across the threshold of the Neville household. Whisky?'

Thornton nodded and added: 'Just a small one, please.'

'Small? That word does not feature in my alcoholic lexicon.' So saying, he handed Thornton a large tumbler of the amber spirit.

'I am intrigued as to why you invited me this evening,' said the policeman, taking a small sip of whisky.

'Not as intrigued as I am as to why you accepted.'

'I am a detective, and as such, I'm a curious cove. My preoccupation is the study of human nature in all its guises. I get many opportunities to observe the lower echelon of society, but it is rare for me to mingle with the rich and aristocratic.'

Darke grinned. 'I had not expected a thesis in response to my little question, but I applaud your reply.'

'Now answer my question.'

'Less noble, I am afraid. I get bored at these parties which, as an artist, I am obliged to attend from time to time. It is as though breeding and money have rotted the brains of those who possess them. Carla usually keeps me tolerably sane, but she is away celebrating her mother's fiftieth birthday at the family seat in Bath. You are my intelligent substitute.'

Thornton chuckled. 'I have no fear about holding an intelligent conversation with you but, compared to Carla, my appearance is a decided disappointment, I am sure.'

'A good omen. We begin the evening by agreeing with each other.'

Some minutes later, the two men were seated in a hansom cab, rattling through the darkening thoroughfares of London en route to Lord Neville's house.

'The fellow lives in great splendour, in a cavern of a place out at Hampstead. It is stuffed with all kinds of large and grotesque artefacts from the colonies – stuffed apes, tigers' heads and the like,' observed Darke with some distaste, as he rummaged inside his overcoat. At length he produced a hip flask and after unscrewing the top, passed it to his companion.

Thornton declined the offer of a drink.

'Permit me to take a gulp then,' said Darke. 'I need extra mental insulation on these occasions.' So saying, he threw his head back and appeared to drain the flask dry. By now, Thornton was used to Darke's habitual large intake of alcohol, and yet he had never seen him drunk or any less than coherent and civil. Nevertheless, Thornton knew that his friend used drink as a crutch, a means by which he coped with a world that to Darke was far more mundane and drab than he believed it should be. To Darke, it seemed, reality was disappointing, and it needed a little help. Alcohol helped to blur the edges and add colour, but he never allowed it to interfere with his own mental focus.

'I get a distinct impression that you hold a particular antipathy towards Lord Neville.'

Darke's eyes flashed in the gloom of the cab. 'Astute as ever, Inspector.'

'As I shall be in his company this evening, it would be useful if you gave me some details regarding the man and his character.'

Darke returned the whisky flask to his overcoat and sat back in his seat, steepling his gloved fingers and placing them to his lips in a moment of contemplation. 'The man and his character, eh? Well, I will try. Lord Anthony Neville is a young man, not yet forty, the sole heir to the Neville fortune. Married to a downtrodden creature, Evelyn. She was a former actress of limited talent, or so

I have been led to understand. The union has produced no children, which may be a blessing, particularly if they were to take after
their father. Although he toyed unsuccessfully with politics when
he was in his twenties, he now has no occupation, save what he
grandly believes is his patronage of the arts. He has dabbled in the
theatre, acting as a financial backer to some productions, I believe.
However, essentially he lives the life of a rich man. An idle rich
man … of the most narcissistic nature.'

'Hence the portrait.'

'Yes. He wanted a permanent record of his charms.' Darke
paused and raised an eyebrow. 'It really should be a miniature.'

Both men grinned.

'I must confess,' continued Darke, 'that I knew little of the fellow
before he began sitting for me, but after a few days I had developed a
bitter dislike of his arrogance, his lack of compassion, intelligence and
his demeaning treatment of servants and, in particular, of his wife.
As a staunch believer in atavism, I am of the opinion that we have in
Neville a throwback to the seventeenth-century aristocrat, the land-
owner who on a whim could have a lazy shepherd hung, drawn and
quartered if it pleased him — and so often it did please him.'

Thornton was surprised at the vehemence of Darke's observations. He knew his companion was a passionate man, but his
passions were usually of a positive nature, flamboyant and full of
unfettered enthusiasm.

'If you feel like this, why did you continue to paint the man?'

'Ah, there is the rub, Thornton, there is the rub. As you know,
I am not a poor man. I could, if I so wish, throw my paints, brushes
and easel out into the gutter and live on my inherited and carefully
invested fortune. But I must have an occupation. I must keep my
mind and spirit busy. And I have promised myself to achieve some
status in the world of art. I started at the bottom of the prodigious
ladder, but now I am off the ground — not to dizzying heights,
you understand — but off the ground. My daubs are appreciated.
My name is gradually becoming known.'

'Known enough for Sir Anthony Neville to secure your services.'

'Precisely. Sir Anthony Neville is another rung on my ladder. He is also a challenge to my nature. If I am to succeed in my chosen pursuit, I cannot let personal feelings interfere with the development of my talent. So I must bite my tongue and drink a little more.' Suddenly, Darke's stern features melted into a grin. 'Bite my tongue, drink a little more – and pocket the large cheque, of course.' He threw back his head in a raucous laugh.

On arriving at Neville's house, which stood on the edge of the dark, forbidding Hampstead common, the two men were led by a liveried flunkey into the salon. This was a large room, almost as spacious as a small ballroom, thought Thornton, which was already filled with guests chatting in informal groups. There were gentlemen attired in various forms of black and white and ladies in opulent gowns, with exotic fans and expansive décolletage.

The air was thick with a grey veil of cigar smoke and the noise of conversation – conversation that at first sounded reasoned and rational, and as Thornton perceived, of a coherent nature. This was Society, then. Here was not of the same nature of chatter heard in the police canteen or the Rose and Crown, where he often took a drink after his day's labours. However, after a while, as he overheard snatches of dialogue from various groups in the room, the policeman was able to judge that these interchanges were in many ways just as empty, facile and insincere. It was just that they were made in smoother tones.

In the far corner, a string quartet played some undistinguished melody which struggled to be heard above the hum of egos being expounded. Meanwhile waiters, almost unobserved, moved around the room with glasses of champagne. These were snatched from the trays with greedy voracity.

On a raised platform situated by the far wall was an easel holding a painting, which was draped in a red velvet cloth to keep it hidden from view.

'The portrait?' enquired Thornton in a whisper, nodding at the easel.

'The portrait,' affirmed Darke. 'Now let's grab a glass before we are spotted.' He beckoned to a waiter, who proffered his tray in order that the two men could help themselves. Darke took two glasses for himself and drained the first before Thornton had time to retrieve his own.

'Good stuff,' observed Darke, placing the empty glass on the departing tray. 'Our host has a fine cellar.'

'My dear Luther, why didn't you let me know you were here?' The voice, whining and high-pitched, came from behind them. The two men turned to face a tall man with broad aristocratic features, framed by rather extravagantly coiffured blonde hair. He was in possession of a weak smile that refused to reveal the teeth.

'Because I have only just arrived,' responded Darke with a graceful bow. 'Lord Neville, allow me to introduce a friend of mine, Edward Thornton.'

Without a word, the two men shook hands limply. Having never seen Neville before, Thornton was surprised how good looking he was. There was a pleasing symmetry to his features that gave the man an air of glamour.

'A fellow artist?' Neville's question was addressed to Luther Darke.

'In a manner of speaking, eh, Edward?'

Before Thornton had time to respond to this mischievous suggestion, Neville took Darke's arm and steered him towards the dais that held the painting. Thornton had only been in the man's company for a few uncomfortable seconds, but the detective already sympathised with Darke's view of Lord Neville. Despite his pleasing looks, there was something sneering, arrogant and dismissive in his demeanour. Certainly as a lowly and unknown friend of Luther Darke, the 'cherished' painter, he had been dismissed with a cursory glance.

Neville was now clapping his hands vigorously to attract attention from the assembled throng. The musicians ceased playing and every eye in the room turned to face him. Like an actor preparing to deliver his favourite speech, he waited until all conversation died.

'My friends, as you know, you have been invited here to witness the unveiling of a great work of art. And it is a great work of art, I can assure you. I know because I have seen it.' There was a pause for a thin murmur of laughter. Neville pulled a decidedly embarrassed-looking Luther Darke closer to him. 'This is the artist, Mr Luther Darke, who has caught the very essence of the painting's subject: me.' He turned with a flourish towards the easel. 'I now have great pleasure unveiling my portrait for all the world to see.'

As Neville took hold of the velvet cloth, the crowd pressed forward, eager to glimpse the painting. Thornton also found himself caught up with the general curiosity. How had Darke treated his subject, he wondered.

With a dramatic tug, Neville pulled the cloth from the easel; it fell to the floor, revealing the portrait. Immediately there were cries of shock and dismay. Initially Neville could not discern the reason for this disturbed reaction, until he turned to gaze upon the portrait and saw the outrage for himself. The canvas had been slashed several times, in such a vicious manner that the face it bore was unrecognisable.

Neville gave a strange bleat of disbelief and stumbled backwards in shock. 'Who has done this thing?' he cried, flinging his arms wide.

There was an immediate response to the question. It came from the back of the salon, where a voice boomed out, 'I have!'

All eyes turned to face the speaker. He was a tall, dark man of medium build, who possessed a mop of limp brown hair combed in a centre parting. He wore shiny round spectacles, which gave him the air of a cleric or scholar. With slow deliberate strides, he began to walk towards the dais and instinctively the hushed crowd parted to allow his passage. This, thought Thornton, is turning out to be a much more interesting evening than I ever anticipated.

On reaching the dais, the man stopped and faced Neville who, on recognising him, gave a cry of horror. 'You! John! But why…?'

'Why?' came the reply, tinged with sardonic disbelief, as the man produced a pistol from his jacket. He held the weapon at arm's length, pointing it directly at the astounded aristocrat. Before the frozen gaze of all onlookers, he appeared to fire the gun directly at Lord Neville's heart. The gunshot resounded in the crowded room and with a sharp agonised cry, Neville clutched his chest. Staggering backwards, his legs gave way beneath him, and he slumped heavily against Darke, causing both men to fall to the ground.

There was immediate pandemonium. With cries of dismay and outrage, men pressed forward to see if they could help; some women shrieked hysterically, while others froze with the shock at what they had seen. With skill and alacrity, Thornton threaded his way through the crowd in search of the gunman. Between the sea of bobbing heads he spied the miscreant making his way to the door.

'Stop him!' shouted Thornton, pointing out the attacker with his outstretched hand. His cry was lost in the general hubbub and, with dismay, he saw his quarry slip from the salon unhindered and unnoticed. Now frantically thrusting people aside, the policeman barged his way forward in order to give chase. Within seconds he was in the vast hallway. To his dismay he found it empty, but he noticed that the main doorway to the house was ajar. As he reached it, a servant came forward, casting a puzzled glance at the open door. Thornton judged from the fellow's expression that he was totally unaware of the events that had just taken place.

'I had no idea that people would be leaving so early,' he intoned solemnly, with some embarrassment. 'May I fetch your hat and coat, sir?'

'Did you see the man leave?' Thornton dragged the servant to the door.

A furrow of unease creased the flunkey's brow. 'I did not, sir. As I remarked, I did not expect that the guests would be leaving…'

But Thornton did not wait to hear the end of the sentence. He sped out into the night and down the winding driveway.

Passing through the large stone gateway, he scanned the road in both directions. There was nothing to be seen. No man. No vehicle. His quarry had disappeared into the darkness.

By the time the inspector had returned to the salon, some order had been established. Neville lay where he had fallen and was being attended to by a doctor. Darke knelt by his side, as did a slim raven-haired woman with pale delicate features and glittering dark eyes that were moist with tears.

On seeing Thornton, Darke rose and took him to one side. 'You'd better telephone for some help, Inspector. My patron is dead.'

Thornton nodded. 'I guessed as much. I chased after the fellow, but he was as quick as an eel. Likely as not he had a carriage waiting.'

'Likely as not.'

'Shot through the heart then, eh?'

'Shot through the painting, actually. Art critics – you meet them everywhere.'

'What do you mean?'

Darke gave a grim laugh. 'I think we've got one for our casebook here, my friend. Sir Anthony Neville was not touched by the bullet. I was close enough to see that just at the last moment our antagonist moved his aim to the portrait – already cut to ribbons – and fired at that. In fact, the bullet hit the rather prodigious frame.' Darke held out his hand to reveal a small, distended pellet. 'I dug it out of the frame just now.'

'Well, I'll be … then how did Neville die?'

Darke turned to look at the prostrate form of Lord Neville which was now being covered by a white sheet. 'He died of a heart attack, old boy. He died of shock!'

A little later, after the police had arrived from Scotland Yard – Inspector Barraclough, an old rival of Thornton's, a sergeant and two constables – Darke lured his friend away from the salon and passed him his hat and coat. 'Time for a little investigation of our own, Edward. Now, now, remember you are off-duty, and what I'm about to suggest will not hinder your erstwhile colleagues.'

'What are you about to suggest?' said Thornton warily, as he tugged on his coat.

'You will recall Neville addressing his would-be assassin as John?'

'Of course.'

'His wife confirmed that the man was indeed John Coram.'

'The actor.'

Darke nodded.

'Well, he certainly knew how to make a grand entrance and a swift exit.'

'Apparently, at one time Neville was involved in backing one of Coram's productions.'

'So we have our man.'

'In a manner of speaking. We know who he is – but you do not yet have him floundering in your net. What charge could you bring? Shooting a painting? This is a nice little mystery indeed. I suggest we call on him this evening. Lady Neville has very kindly furnished me with his address. Are you game?'

Some ten minutes later, as the chimes of Big Ben were announcing the hour of ten o'clock, the two men were standing on the steps of a very smart town house in Carisbroke Gardens, Chelsea, the home of John Coram. Darke rang the bell, and the door was answered by a tall, dark-haired young man who although not dressed for the part, appeared to be the butler. He registered some surprise at receiving visitors at this hour of the evening.

'We should like to see your master, Mr John Coram,' announced Luther Darke, moving forward as to enter the house. However, the servant barred his way.

'I am afraid that is not possible. Mr Coram is engaged in dining with friends at present.'

At this point Thornton moved forward and tapped the servant firmly on the shoulder. 'I am Inspector Thornton of Scotland Yard. My colleague and I are involved in an investigation of a heinous murder which has taken place this evening, and it is imperative that we interview Mr Coram at once. Now I am sure you do not want to place yourself in the position of being arrested for hindering the course of justice.'

The servant blanched at these hard words.

'Now,' continued the policeman in the same manner, 'I suggest you announce us to your master, or...'

He spoke no more, for the servant had already retreated into the hallway and beckoned them to enter. Without a word he led the two men down the dark oak-panelled hallway and into a small, gloomy candle-lit dining room where a fire burned low in the hearth. There were three people seated at the table: the first, an elderly man, with a mane of pure white hair that cascaded about his shoulders. He looked up at the visitors with large rheumy eyes that peered out at them through thick, wire-rimmed spectacles. The second diner was a feminine-faced young man, with black button eyes and the faint suggestion of a moustache under his slender aquiline nose. At the head of the table was the man Darke and Thornton had seen earlier that evening: John Coram. Despite the dim and shadowy illumination, Thornton was in no doubt. The fellow was dressed in the same dark clothes. His spectacles caught the candlelight as he turned to face the unexpected guests. Unlike the other two diners he did not seem surprised or inconvenienced by their sudden appearance.

'What is it, Simon?' he asked casually.

The servant began to explain the intrusion: 'I am sorry sir, but these men are from the police...'

'Good gracious.' This exclamation came from the white-haired man, who dabbed his mouth with his napkin in some consternation.

Coram rose to his feet. 'You are bid welcome to the feast,' he cried. 'Simon, bring chairs for our guests. They have missed the victuals, but they can certainly join us for the brandy and cigars.'

'By Jove, brandy would slip down a treat,' said Darke affably. 'Don't you think so, Edward?'

The policeman nodded reluctantly. He decided to follow Darke's lead in this charade for a while to see where it would lead them.

Chairs were brought and brandies poured before the conversation continued.

'Now then, gentlemen, long days and warm nights to you,' Coram cried, raising his glass and taking a drink. 'Ah, that is an excellent brandy, even if I say so myself.'

'Mr Coram,' Thornton said brusquely, irritated by the actor's nonchalance. 'We have just come from the home of Sir Anthony Neville.'

'My, you are doing the rounds tonight.'

The young diner with the incipient moustache sniggered.

'What my friend is intimating,' said Darke, 'is that while we have come from Lord Neville's this evening, we know that so have you.'

Coram rocked back in his chair with laughter. 'The Devil I have. You would not get me under that scoundrel's roof for all the greasepaint in Stratford. I have not left my own home and hearth this night.'

'Lord Neville is dead, Mr Coram.'

The actor's face froze in mid grin. 'Is this the truth?'

'Of course it is. You know it is.'

Coram shook his head in disbelief. 'I know nothing of the kind. I disliked the man intensely, but I would not wish him dead. There's more pain in the living ... but why do you come here with this news and ... intimate that I already know?'

'You attempted to shoot Lord Neville this evening at his home. You were seen by around thirty witnesses.'

'What bloody nonsense!' This outburst came from the youth.

'Calm yourself, Ralph,' Coram said. 'It is for me to sort this matter out. Now, sir, who exactly are you?'

'I am Inspector Thornton of Scotland Yard.'

'And your friend?'

'I am Luther Darke…'

'The painter?'

Darke raised his glass in acknowledgement. 'Amongst other things.'

'Now, gentlemen, you know who I am. Allow me to introduce you to my dining companions. This is Ralph Trevelyan, a fellow actor and close friend. And this gentleman is none other than His Reverence, Horatio Fisher, the Bishop of London.'

At the mention of his name the old gentlemen pulled away his napkin, and in the dim light Thornton and Darke observed the purple smock beneath his jacket and the insignia of his office. 'Good evening, gentlemen,' he said quietly, obviously somewhat confused as to what was happening.

'Now, Inspector, both these gentlemen can vouch that I have not left this house all evening. Indeed, for the last two and a half hours we have been engaged in dining on a sumptuous four-course repast. Is that not correct, Your Reverence?'

Both Thornton and Darke turned to the aged cleric for confirmation. The Bishop nodded. 'Guinea fowl of the tastiest variety, cooked in its own juices. An excellent meal.'

Thornton frowned in disbelief. 'But I saw you with my very eyes fire a gun at Lord Neville just over an hour ago.'

'Just over an hour ago we had just about finished our hors d'oeuvres: oysters.'

'I also saw you at Lord Neville's.' Darke spoke softly, but his tone was more direct and challenging.

Coram shook his head, still smiling, but the humour had departed from his eyes. They glinted harshly in the candlelight. 'You did not see me, my painter friend. Someone like me, perchance. At what time was I supposed to be playing Banquo's ghost to Neville's Macbeth?'

'At nine o' clock.'

'We sat down to dine at seven-thirty, and I have only left this room briefly on two occasions, to visit my cellar to select another bottle of wine. Is that not correct, Your Grace?'

Instinctively the Bishop glanced over to the large grandfather clock in the corner. 'Oh, yes, that is correct. I remember commenting on the charming chimes on each hour – eight, nine and ten. Gentlemen, I believe you have made a grave mistake. Whatever unfortunate incident took place this evening, Mr Coram can in no way be implicated. Quite simply, he has been here all evening.'

'There you are, gentlemen, the Church verifies my innocence.'

There was a long pause, filled only by the gentle ticking of the grandfather clock.

'Surely, there is no more to be said,' observed Coram at length. 'There has been a grave misunderstanding … on your part.'

'I think we have gone as far with this business as we are able tonight,' said Thornton, with a frustration he barely concealed, 'but I know what I saw. The matter is not at an end. I am sure I shall have the need to interview you three gentlemen in more detail at a later date.'

'I am always happy to assist the police,' said the Bishop, 'but I cannot think I have anything to add to my reassurance that we sat down to dine at seven-thirty, after which Mr Coram left the room on two occasions and returned within five minutes or so.'

Luther Darke stirred the coals in the grate until flames broke through, stretching their yellow tongues and sending shadows dancing on the walls of the room.

'Another five minutes and we'll have a jolly blaze. In the meantime, drop your coat and pull up a chair, Edward.'

'I'm not sure I can sit down at present. I am so angry I need to … move around.'

'Be my guest.' Darke threw his arms out as an invitation to his friend to use the whole sitting room for his perambulations if he wished. The two men caught each other's eyes and broad smiles resulted.

It was nearly midnight now, and instinctively they had returned to Darke's house in Manchester Square for a 'post-mortem' of the evening's events. They had exchanged barely a word since leaving John Coram's house until now. During the cab ride, Darke had retreated into thought but Edward Thornton had been too disturbed, too frustrated, for his mental faculties to work rationally.

'A further nightcap, old boy?' Darke's hand hovered over the decanter of brandy. He had already poured himself a generous measure.

As though to defy his own innate reserve, Thornton nodded decisively. 'And make it a large one.'

'My, the actor has pierced your skin somewhat.'

'You know as well as I, that we saw him at Lord Neville's house tonight. It was John Coram who fired that gun.'

'Of course it was,' agreed Darke, handing Thornton his drink. 'That is not in question. Now, for goodness sake, do sit down before you wear out my rather expensive Indian carpet.'

The inspector did as he was bidden.

Darke sat by the fire, cradling his glass in both hands. Within moments of him settling in the chair, a cat leapt upon his lap and curled itself into a ball. Darke stroked the creature absentmindedly until it purred contentedly. 'A murder has been done. A very clever and calculated murder. It is the whys, hows and wherefores that we need to sort out. Let us suppose that we could prove Master Coram was the gunman at Neville's house tonight. Of what crime would he be guilty? Shooting at a picture frame. That does not carry a very heavy penalty. I mean … Coram could not be sure that such an act of vandalism would bring about his lordship's demise – or could he?'

'You are losing me,' said Thornton, draining his glass.

'Just as Coram expected. He has included so many twists and turns in this particular game…'

'Game! Murder isn't a game…' The words were now slurred and Thornton's eyelids were beginning to droop.

'Oh, it is a game – theatrical in nature, as it should be when designed by such a talented actor as Coram, but a game nonetheless. It is only a matter of deciphering the rules. Let me say this now: I am convinced Coram planned Neville's demise and planned it in such a way that celebrated the art of theatre – the art of illusion. After all, the stage is the ultimate deception.'

He turned to his friend for a response to this declaration, but his eyes were closed and his bosom was heaving in the easy rhythm of sleep. Darke smiled gently and stared into the revived flames in the grate as ideas and concepts began to formulate within his own brain. 'I have it – but it is not engendered yet,' he muttered to himself, before taking another gulp of brandy.

When Edward Thornton woke in the morning, he found himself lying on the sofa in Darke's sitting room, with a blanket over him and a cat curled up at his feet. Already the grey light of dawn was filtering through the gaps in the drawn curtains. Without thinking, he threw off the blanket and jumped up. The cat squawked angrily at being disturbed so roughly and sought refuge under the sofa.

Thornton stood uncertainly, while the room around him shuddered. The very furniture seemed to vibrate, a sensation that was accompanied by a sudden throbbing in his temples. He slumped back down on the sofa, taking account of the other symptoms that were now manifesting themselves: the dry throat, the blurred vision and the aching limbs. He recollected it all from his youthful days: this was the emperor of a hangover. Just as he had successfully made this deduction, there came a tap at the door and Darke's manservant George entered. He was carrying a tray that contained a silver coffee-pot and a large mug.

'The master thought that you would be in need of a strong brew this morning, sir,' he intoned softly, placing the tray down on a table near to Thornton.

'The master was right.'

'I have found that he invariably is. Will that be all?'

Thornton glanced at his watch. It was nine o'clock. 'Indeed. Perhaps you would alert Mr Darke that I am awake and due to leave shortly.'

'The master has already gone out, sir. About half an hour ago. He asked me to give you this.'

George passed the inspector a cream envelope and then withdrew. Thornton tore open the envelope and read the missive within:

Morning, Mon Brave,

No doubt you are a little dismayed this morning concerning the events of last night – dismayed and somewhat delicate about the head. But nil desperandum. We shall soon set matters right.

Meet me for lunch at Enrico's in Saxe-Coburg Square at 12.30 and I shall recount my morning's adventures.

Luther.

Darke's morning adventures began with an early visit to Covent Garden Market to pick up a large bunch of white lilies, which later he presented to Lady Neville when he called upon her to pay his condolences.

'How terribly sweet of you, Mr Darke,' she said, after instructing a maid to take them and put them in water. She then bade her visitor sit by her on the chaise longue.

'Your husband was a remarkable man.'

'In some ways, yes. I find myself in a terrible situation this morning…' She turned her head slightly as though she was embarrassed to reveal her emotions to a man she hardly knew.

'The death of a loved one is always a tragedy.'

'Ah, there you touch the nub of the dilemma, Mr Darke. The death of a loved one is indeed always a tragedy; the same cannot always be said of the death of a husband.'

'I am sorry, I'm not quite sure that I understand you,' Darke responded softly, understanding fully.

Lady Neville paused for a moment, uncertainty clouding her face. Nervously she smoothed her dress while she seemed to be summoning up the courage to say what she wanted to say. And then suddenly she turned to Darke, looking him directly in the face. 'In the time you spent in this house, you must have observed a certain coolness between my husband and I.'

Darke gave a gentle nod.

'Whatever fiery passion that had flamed between us when we first were married had long since died away. Simply, I did not love my husband. He did not love me. Please forgive me for being so frank with you, Mr Darke. It is so much easier to confess such unhappy truths to a comparative stranger. I suppose I should feel something like guilt now that Anthony is dead, but all that I do feel is … relief. That makes me a terrible woman, doesn't it?'

'Certainly not.' Darke rose and moved to the window. Lifting a rose from the vase on the sill, he held it to his nose. 'This flower is honest. What it gives the world is colour, beauty and fragrance. It promises less and somehow gives more. It would be terrible to pretend affection, grief and true mourning where none existed. I knew your husband for only a few short weeks, but I learned in that time that he was not a loveable man.'

'Now I have confessed my secret, I hope that as a gentleman you will keep it for me. It benefits no one if it becomes public knowledge that ours was a loveless marriage.'

'Certainly.' Darke returned and sat beside Lady Neville. He gazed into her pale face with more care. She was, he now realised, a handsome creature. Her fragile beauty had been somewhat disguised by her diffidence. He placed the rose into her hand. 'It shall be as you wish. But forgive me if I press you on a few details concerning your husband's death.'

'Ah! Have the police apprehended the scoundrel Coram yet?'

'They are investigating the matter, but his actions, although reprehensible...'

'He as good as murdered Anthony.'

'Why do you say that?'

'Coram knew of my husband's heart condition. Any violent shock...'

'How did he know? What grudge did the actor hold against Lord Neville?'

She sighed. 'It is common knowledge in theatrical circles that Anthony was to be the main financial backer of a new play that John Coram was to direct, but on a whim, my husband pulled out at the last moment. As result, the play was never performed and Coram lost a small fortune.'

'Am I correct in thinking that this whim was based on your husband's discovery that you intended to return to the stage and appear in this play?'

Lady Neville hesitated a moment before nodding in agreement. 'I was his property. That's how he regarded me. I had to be kept in my cage. He wasn't prepared to share me with anyone. And of course, as his wife, he would not tolerate me degrading myself, as he termed it, by appearing once more on a theatrical stage.'

'Coram must have been bitterly disappointed to lose both his backing and his leading lady in one fell swoop.'

'I suppose so.'

'Did he threaten your husband on any previous occasion that you know of?'

Lady Neville shook her head.

'Do you think that Coram was responsible for the mutilation of the portrait?'

'It would seem logical.'

'But when could he have done it? I was led to believe that it was to be kept in your husband's private study until the unveiling.'

'So it was. He guarded it jealously. He was very pleased with it. He said you had captured his true nobility.'

'Did he? And what did you think?'

'I? I thought nothing. I never saw the portrait. You and he were the only persons to see it. He brought it from his study – covered by a cloth – himself when the party began. He would let no one else near it.'

'There was one other person to see the painting: the vandal who destroyed it.'

'Yes, of course.'

Darke rose and gave a brief bow. 'I have taken up too much of your time already, Lady Neville. You have been kind to confide in me.'

The lady rose and shook Darke's hand. 'Thank you for being so understanding.'

'One more question, if I may, before I leave. How long had your husband suffered with a weak heart?'

'His condition was diagnosed about two years ago. He saw several eminent doctors hoping that one would say it was all a mistake – but they didn't.'

'How was he treated?'

'By drugs. He had tablets to take to stabilise his condition. Three a day, more if he felt weak or agitated.'

'I see. Thank you again.'

With that, Darke left Lady Neville, still clutching the rose, a lonely figure in the great drawing room. 'How wonderfully theatrical,' he muttered to himself under his breath as he collected his hat and stick.

Enrico's was already busy when Edward Thornton entered. The large dining room was almost full. The clientele was predominantly male. Thornton espied Darke almost immediately. He was ensconced at a table by the window, a half-consumed bottle of white wine before him. He rose from his chair at the inspector's approach. 'Glad you could come, my dear fellow. I hope the head has cleared up.'

'Cleared up and clearly thinking.'

'Oh, really.' Darke raised a brow. 'You have news?'

'I have news, and no doubt so have you.'

'A little.'

The two men smiled.

'Well sit down, Edward, and let's exchange the gossip. Your smile and demeanour intrigue me.'

Glancing around at his surroundings with an awkward uneasiness, Thornton did as he was bidden. 'This looks rather an expensive establishment. I'm not sure my policeman's pay can run to…'

Darke waved his hands to banish Thornton's words. 'The lunch is on me, of course. Now let me tell you what I've been doing this a.m., and then you can reciprocate.'

So saying, Darke recounted his interview with Lady Neville. With his remarkable facility for remembering conversation and mimicry he played the scene out for the policeman. It was an edited version, in which certain revelations were held back in order for Darke to use them later with a more dramatic flourish. Neither did he comment on what the lady had said, nor did he embroider any of her responses. He wanted his friend to reach his own conclusions.

After Darke had finished, he drained his glass dry and summoned a waiter to order another bottle while Thornton inwardly digested the information he had just been given.

'The trout for me,' Luther Darke announced grandly, as the waiter uncorked the wine. 'What about you, Edward?'

'What…? Oh, I haven't had a chance to study the menu. Trout, you say? That sounds fine.'

'Excellent. Fish is good for the grey matter and we need to be on sparkling form today – rather like this jolly hock. Pass your glass and try some for yourself. Now, old sleuth hound, what truffles have you dug up for our delectation?'

'John Coram.'

'Don't tell me he's signed a confession – or that the Bishop of London we saw last night was a fake.'

'Neither, but I have learned things which increase my certainty of his guilt.'

'Pray tell.'

'One of the narks I use is a character called Stage Door Sammy. He's a cove who can give you the lowdown on every theatrical performance and performer in London.'

Darke's eyes brightened with interest.

'I got in touch with Sammy this morning to see what he could tell me about our slippery customer, Mr Coram. He came up with some very interesting information. As we already know, Lord Neville was due to back his play about the reformation, *Angels and Anthems*, when he decided against it.'

Darke nodded. 'Don't tell me that he had some objections concerning the religious content?'

'I doubt it. But I suspect that you were not aware that Lady Neville was due to play the lead. It was to be her return to the stage.'

'Indeed. The stuff of romantic novels, my dear Thornton. Bored with her loveless marriage, she yearned for her former glories in theatre as Evelyn Porter. Evelyn Porter was her stage name, I believe.'

'Yes. But when Lord Neville learned that Coram and his good wife had once been lovers, he brought the curtain down somewhat prematurely on the venture.'

'Lovers, eh? Now that is news, Edward.'

'Yes. Interesting isn't it?'

'Certainly – but why does it not surprise me, I wonder?'

'Things are shaping up. So we have Lady Neville robbed of her part, and Coram of his play.'

'It establishes a motive for revenge for two parties. An excellent morning's work, Inspector. One assumes that now his lordship is dead, Lady Neville will inherit the family boodlebag and therefore be in a position to bail Coram out and buy a new set of greasepaints for herself.'

Thornton grinned. 'The case is as good as solved … except for one little difficulty.'

Darke lifted his glass and took a sip of wine. 'We have to prove how it was done.'

Thornton's grin faded and he emitted a sigh. 'Yes … that was the little difficulty I had in mind.'

'Don't worry too much about that. Certainly don't allow it to spoil your lunch. Any knot, no matter how cunningly tied, can be untied again. Just answer me this question: where is Lord Neville's body now?'

'In the police mortuary at the yard.'

'Will the clothes he was wearing when he died be there also?'

'Certainly.'

'Excellent. Well, the police mortuary it is for us after lunch which, if I am not mistaken, is heading towards our table at this very moment. *Bon appetit*, Inspector.'

The police mortuary, situated at the rear of the new headquarters of Scotland Yard, was a dreary building, cold and forbidding. Despite having the modern convenience of electric lighting, the rooms inside were gloomy and drab.

The attendant led Thornton and Darke to the 'keeping room' where dead bodies were stored up to a week after death before they were prepared for burial or cremation.

'I have no wish to reacquaint myself with his lordship,' said Darke as the three men entered the chamber. 'I just want a chance to examine his clothes – in particular his waistcoat.'

The attendant cast him curious glance. 'Fancy one like it, do you, sir?'

'Certainly not. It was far too vulgar.'

The attendant gave a shrug. 'I thought Inspector Barraclough was handling this case,' he said pointedly, as he retrieved a sack from a large cupboard standing near the door. 'Property of Lord Anthony Neville, aged thirty-seven. Cause of death: heart attack.'

'We don't need a recital. Just pass us the sack and then you may leave us,' Thornton said sharply.

The attendant stiffened and with a surly, 'Yes, sir,' he did as he was bidden. Darke fell upon the sack, and within moments he had extracted the green and grey striped waistcoat. With care Darke dipped his fingers into one of the waistcoat pockets and retrieved a small silver case. On opening the case, he revealed its contents to Thornton: three small pink pills.

'During the course of sitting for me, I saw Lord Neville take out this pill box every two hours or so and pop one of these pink devils in his mouth.'

'His medication.'

'According to Lady Neville, they controlled his heartbeat and helped to maintain its very weak equilibrium.'

'I see, and yet I do not see. How does this help our case?'

'We cannot be sure that it does until we have them analysed. Now I happen to know a brilliant chemist, Dr Oliver Drysdale … he's but a short cab ride away in Harley Street.'

An hour later, after an illuminating visit to Dr Oliver Drysdale, Darke and Thornton were in a hansom on their way to Coram's Chelsea address.

'To use the parlance of the theatre, we are now into the last act,' observed Darke.

Thornton grimaced. 'I was well up with you and the case until we got to the blasted pills, Luther. Now I find I'm plunged into the darkness again. Will you please explain?'

'Not fully, old chap. I don't want that prize brain of yours to atrophy through lack of use. Let's tease some theorising from you. Now we are agreed that Lady Neville, our star actress, Evelyn Porter, and her ex-lover, John Coram, are responsible for the clever murder of Lord Anthony Neville.'

'Absolutely. Although I am not so sure that the prefix "ex" is quite accurate under the circumstances.'

'Yes. You are probably right. Our two murderous thespians have been clever in committing a murder without there appearing to have been a murder committed. Neville was not shot, hung, stabbed or poisoned. He died of a heart attack, brought on by over-excitement and fright caused by his beloved portrait being slashed to ribbons and a man apparently about to shoot him.'

'There's no doubt about it. Shock and fear.'

'But how could they be absolutely certain that these events would cause Neville's demise?'

Thornton's mouth dropped open. 'The pills! Of course, the pills!'

'Daylight, eh?'

The inspector rubbed his hands with delight. 'Lady Neville substituted his medication – his life-stabilising medication – for … what did Doctor Drysdale call them? Placebos?'

'Exactly,' grinned Darke, rubbing his hands. 'Dummy pills with no medical properties whatsoever. Unbeknownst to him, Neville's condition had been worsening daily. His heart was very weak and unprotected. The ruined portrait and the apparent attack upon his person were too much for that damaged pumping station. It burst.'

'The cold-hearted villains.'

'But clever ones, Edward. They must have felt confident that no one would question Neville's actual death by heart attack, only the dramatic events that led up to it. Her ladyship was remarkably honest and forthcoming in her interview with me this morning. I suspect she thought that her candid responses to my questions made her appear all the more innocent and that no hint of suspicion would fall on her. Then there is our actor-manager,

Mr Coram. Even if it could be proved that he was the person who fired the gun – all he did was fire at the portrait. But between them, our pretty pair constructed a watertight alibi for Coram, one that is corroborated by none other than the Bishop of London. They have, or so they believe, sealed up every avenue of detection. Coram is the innocent murderer.'

'You know differently.'

'I do and, if you apply yourself, you should reach the same conclusion as I have. Think, Edward, how is it possible for a man to be in two places at once: at dinner at home and intruding upon a private party to fire a gun and frighten the host to death?'

'It is not possible.'

'Precisely.'

On reaching the home of John Coram, Darke and Thornton learned that the man they were seeking was at the Cockpit Theatre. Another cab journey brought them to this establishment, a gloomy soot-encrusted property located just off Marylebone Road. Although the front of the building was bolted and in darkness, they discovered an elderly man by the stage door who announced himself to be the caretaker. He informed them that Mr Coram was in his office, which could be reached by means of a spiral staircase located behind the backcloth.

The interior of the theatre was dimly illuminated. There was an odd gas lamp here and there to throw a pale amber glow into the sepulchral gloom, and daylight speared in through an occasional grimy window, but darkness pressed in on the visitors as though it was challenging their unwelcome presence.

'The land of shadows,' observed Darke as they began to ascend the spiral staircase.

On reaching the top, they found themselves on a gangway above the flies, at the end of which was a small box-like structure:

Coram's office. They could see him through the small window, a candle illuminating his face. He was oblivious of their presence and appeared to be writing furiously.

As the two men entered the tiny, cramped office, Coram glanced up in shock. He dropped his pen and half-rose from his chair, his mouth opening as though he was about to utter something. Then, almost miraculously, he recaptured his composure and nonchalantly slipped back into his seat. Coram's eyes held the two men in a cool gaze, while his lips fashioned themselves into a smile.

A resourceful actor indeed, thought Luther Darke.

'Ah, the inspector and the painter man. You have come to beard me in my den. I would offer you a seat, but as you can see there are none.'

'Concerning the events of last evening, there are some little details that we need to clear up,' said Thornton coolly.

'Oh, that again. I had a visit from your man Barraclough this morning. I seem to have satisfied him with my version of events and by now I am sure he has spoken to the Bishop, who will have done likewise.'

'I am sure Inspector Barraclough is satisfied, Mr Coram, because you present a very plausible story, which is verified by an unimpeachable witness. However, you must remember that I was at Lord Neville's house last evening and I saw you. I did not see your double or someone who resembled you. I saw you!'

Any softness of expression faded from Coram's countenance. 'Then you are going to have to prove it, aren't you Inspector?'

It was Thornton's turn to smile. 'With Mr Darke's help, I think I can.'

'With Mr Darke's help ... oh, painter man turns policeman.'

'We seem to have interrupted you working on your play *Angels and Anthems*,' said Darke, indicating the pile of papers on the desk.

'Why, yes. There are some minor revisions ... nothing more.'

'Preparing the text ready for production.'

'Of course. That is why I invited the Bishop of London to dine with me last evening. There were some ecclesiastical points I wished to clarify. I want my text to be accurate.'

'When is the play to be performed?'

'Soon.'

'Soon, now that you can rely on funding provided by your leading lady.'

'Mr Darke, I do not think it is incumbent upon me to discuss my professional business arrangements with you or the inspector… so if you have nothing further to say …'

'Oh, but I have. As a man of the theatre I thought you would be interested in a little scenario that I have devised myself – a dramatic plot which has all the elements of a crowd-pleaser. The characters you already know. My Lady Neville, her vain and arrogant husband Lord Neville, and an unscrupulous actor.'

'I do not have to listen to this …!'

'I think that you do,' said Thornton, leaning against the door.

'You and Lady Neville, Evelyn Porter, planned the murder of Lord Neville between you,' began Darke, 'although I believe that it was you who constructed the clever dramatic elements of it. It pleased your sense of theatre. Drama in everything, eh? Even murder. Neither of you could bring yourselves to kill the man outright, so his death had to occur by some other means. You decided that he should die of a heart attack. Lady Neville would substitute the pills he required for his heart condition with ineffective fakes, and you would provide the required shock that his weakened heart could not survive. And this is where your love of dramatics really took over and the plot became somewhat complicated. Last night you took the starring role. You strode into the room just as Neville was about to unveil his portrait – which your pretty accomplice had slashed to ribbons only hours before. You knew that Neville would see this desecration as a personal attack upon his person and his beauty, but you could not be sure the shock of this would be great enough to see him off. The gunshot would, though.

Although you changed your aim at the last second, you knew your victim would feel certain the bullet was meant for him. Your ruse worked perfectly. Neville's heart stopped and his fortune passed to your leading lady, who would not only bail out your debts – which I gather are considerable – but finance the production of your new play and star in it as well.'

There was a moment's silence and then Coram began to clap his hands slowly in mock applause. The candle on his desk wavered, sending eerie shadows darting erratically around the walls of the office. 'Very good, Darke. Almost convincing. But there are gaping holes in your theory. If what you say is true, how was it that I have witnesses to say that I was elsewhere at the time?'

'I was coming to that,' said Darke steadily. 'The round trip from your house to Lord Neville's would take you about twenty minutes or so – perhaps less with a good mount. You were in his lordship's house no more than five minutes – just enough time to make your startling entrance, fire the shot and disappear. So a rough estimate suggests that you needed to be absent from your own house for only about thirty minutes – no more, I would have said.'

'But I wasn't absent from my house.'

'The Bishop acknowledged that you left the room on two occasions.'

'To fetch some wine. There were some special vintages I wished him to try. I am very proud of my cellar.'

'It was on the occasion of these absences that you swapped places with your servant. Your servant, Simon, who is also an actor, one of your company, and very used to playing parts. On our arrival last night, despite the dim lighting, I noticed traces of make-up on his face and red indentations on the bridge of his nose where he had been wearing spectacles. He had been wearing spectacles – in order to look like you. He also has your build and bearing. I am sure if we searched your house, we should find a duplicate set of clothes and a wig. After your first absence, supposedly to visit the wine cellar, Simon returned to the dining room some five minutes later impersonating you. Meanwhile, you had raced off to commit murder. As an actor, the servant could comfortably pass himself off as the great John Coram for twenty minutes or so in a very dimly lighted room with an aged cleric in possession of poor eyesight and who had been plied with many glasses of wine. There was also your other accomplice, Ralph, who no doubt engaged the Bishop in long rambling conversations in order to take his attention away from the host, who would be certain to keep his face in the shadows. After the requisite interval, the fake John Coram left the room supposedly to collect yet another bottle of wine, and then you swapped places with him and returned once more, clutching said bottle, to take your seat at the dining table. And the Bishop was none the wiser. Thus you had secured what you believed to be a watertight alibi. But I am afraid, my friend, that it has sprung a leak.'

During Luther Darke's exposition, Coram's face had paled until all the colour had drained from it.

'I feel sure that when pressed, your accomplices will corroborate my version of events. You were so certain that your plan was foolproof that you never seriously considered the possibility of them being questioned, did you?'

'Damn you, painter man!' Coram cried, pulling open a drawer in the desk from which he snatched up a pistol. Flinging his chair over backwards, he jumped to his feet, waving the gun at the two men. 'This time I won't miss if either of you get in my way. Now Inspector, move away from the door.'

Thornton did as he was bidden, but as Coram was about to pass through the doorway, the policeman stuck out his boot, causing the actor to stumble forward and land face downward on the gangway outside. The gun sprang from his grasp and skittered along the planking, slipping over the edge and falling to the stage, some forty feet below. In an instant Coram was on his feet and racing towards the spiral staircase but, before reaching it, he stumbled again. This time, he fell sideways against the wooden parapet, which cracked and splintered under his weight. His eyes widened with terror as he realised what was about to happen. He gave an inarticulate cry of horror as his body teetered for an instant and then he began to fall backwards.

Darke raced down the gangway as Coram slipped over the edge. His arm shot out and grabbed the actor's sleeve just in time to snatch him back from the abyss. A sliver of wood floated down and landed gently on the stage. Coram's feet slithered on the edge for a moment before finding purchase. Thornton also came to his aid and, with the two men's assistance, the actor landed on the gangway once more.

'Come along, Coram,' said Inspector Thornton, pulling out a pair of handcuffs.

The actor looked up at him, his face without expression. 'It seems that our revels now are ended,' he said softly, pulling himself to his feet.

That evening Luther Darke sat holding a whisky glass and stroking his cat, Persephone, staring into the flickering flames of the fire in his sitting room. He thought of Carla and of her return the following day. He smiled at the prospect of their reunion and then his mind returned in its melancholic way to the death of Lord Neville and to his two murderers. He almost felt sorry for them. He knew that they had committed a terrible crime, but in some ways Lord Neville, in the manner of his living, had contributed to his own death. No doubt a sharp lawyer would place great emphasis on the extenuating circumstances with regards to Evelyn Porter, the badly used wife, and she would end up with a brief prison sentence. There would be no such leniency for John Coram. 'What a fool the man has been,' Darke murmured softly, as though he was addressing his cat. 'A fellow of great talent and ingenuity. If he had used his brain in a positive way, rather than resorting to revenge and murder … now only the gallows await.'

Darke took a drink, attempting to banish this sour thought from his mind. The whisky burned his throat in a pleasing way and he sighed. 'We are such stuff as dreams are made on, and our little life is rounded with a sleep,' he said softly, stroking the cat.

Persephone purred contentedly, lost in her own feline dreams.

3

THE MYSTERY OF THE MISSING BLACK PEARL

She took the pearl from its velvet bag and carried it to the window, where she held it up against the pane. The pale winter light endowed it with a cold lustrous sheen that seemed to enhance its dark beauty. 'Oh, you are exquisite,' she cooed. 'Absolutely exquisite.' And overcome by the beauty of the pearl, she kissed it gently. 'I don't know what I should do if I ever lost you.'

Although the day was only just creeping past noon, the sky was already a twilight grey and was now speckled with flakes of snow. Luther Darke tugged his coat around him and shivered as he turned up the astrakhan collar so that it brushed comfortingly against his cheek. He pulled a miserable face at his companion in the carriage. Carla, who was well used to these petulant moods which came upon him when he felt pressured into doing something that he did not want to do, just grinned back at him.

'More snow,' he groaned, casting a glance out of the carriage window.

'Barrington Hall is so pretty in the snow. We can make a snow-man in the garden.'

Darke's features softened into a smile. 'I'd prefer to make love in the boudoir.'

Carla chuckled and gave him a playful slap on the knee. 'Only if you're a good boy,' she said.

'I'm sorry I'm a bore,' he said, taking her hand.

A bore was the last thing Luther Darke could be, but she was not about to tell him that. 'You should not have agreed to paint Lady Harcourt's portrait if you couldn't stomach a trip to the country.'

'It isn't a trip to the country that I detest, it's the thought of staying the weekend in a draughty old hall in the bleak mid-winter having to be polite to a group of people I don't know and with whom I shall have nothing in common. I only agreed to the project in the first place because Lady Harcourt is your godmother. I assumed that she would come up to town for the initial sittings.'

'Isabel is the perfect hostess and Barrington Hall is far from a draughty old pile. You will find it warm and welcoming.'

Darke glanced out of the carriage window. 'It will need to be, if this snow keeps up. Well, my love, as my fate is sealed, perhaps you will give me a resumé of the ghastly guests with whom we shall be incarcerated this weekend.'

Carla could not help being amused at her lover's cynical pessimism knowing, as she did, that most of it was an act. 'Well, there's Isabel, of course, Lady Harcourt. She's a widow, as you know. Her brother Sebastian Carew lives with her and acts as estate manager. The other guests include Walter Palmer. He is an eminent jeweller and has been commissioned to design a setting for Isabel's Black Pearl.'

'Ah, the famous Black Pearl. The biggest and the blackest, I gather, and no doubt the most valuable.'

'Priceless, I should say.'

'Pointless label. Everything has a price. Who else?'

'Isabel's children: Sophie and Randall. Both in their twenties. Randall is the elder by two years, I think. Sophie is married to Gareth Swailes. He's a poet.'

'And a bad one. I have read some of his trite outpourings. And Randall...?'

'A stockbroker.'

'No stimulating intellectual conversation there then. Anyone else?'

Carla hesitated. 'It is likely that Anthony Cushing will be in attendance. He is a near neighbour. A gentleman farmer.'

Darke wrinkled his nose. 'A contradiction in terms, surely.'

Carla ignored the insult. 'I believe he has set his cap at Isabel.'

'Has he, by Jove. That could be fun. I love a romance. Is that the lot?'

'Oh, there's also a rather foul-tempered oaf of a fellow who is likely to be there. Professes to be a painter of sorts, but I've seen his work and he's clearly without talent.'

Darke lunged at Carla, grabbing her round the waist and kissing her full on the lips. 'Just you wait until I get you into that boudoir.'

Isabel Harcourt unlocked the bureau, and from one of the small drawers withdrew a grey velvet bag. She emptied the contents out onto her palm: a large lustrous black pearl, the size of a plump grape. It glinted magnificently in the candlelight. She held it out for her companion to inspect.

Walter Palmer, the jeweller, gave a gasp of admiration and leaned closer to examine the pearl. 'I am surprised that you do not have a more secure housing for such a precious object – a safe perhaps.'

'Nonsense, Mr Palmer. A safe is the first place a thief would look if I were ever burgled.'

'May I?' Palmer's fingers hovered over the pearl.

'Yes, of course.'

Gently, Palmer plucked the pearl from her hand and, holding it up to the light, examined it with an eyeglass. 'I expected a beautiful object, but nothing so magnificent. It is truly remarkable.'

Lady Harcourt smiled and blushed a little as though he were referring to her beauty rather than the pearl's. 'I hope it will inspire you to create the perfect complement for it – a setting that will enhance its unique qualities. Nothing ostentatious that will detract from its perfection, mind you. I do so wish to wear it so that others can appreciate its special qualities.'

'Rest assured, Lady Harcourt,' Palmer said with a smile, 'I am inspired.'

While this conversation was taking place, Isabel Harcourt's daughter Sophie and her husband Gareth were taking tea in the drawing room. Gareth stood by the large French windows which looked on to a small private garden. He gazed out, watching with lazy fascination the relentless flakes of snow swirling down and layering the lawn and softening the contours of the bushes with a thick white cover.

'When are you going to ask her?' he said softly, almost under his breath, his eyes never leaving the flurry of the snow beyond the glass.

'Oh, for heaven's sake, Gar. We've only just got here. I have to pick my moment.'

His features stiffened. 'If we don't get the money…'

'I know, I know. But mother said that last time was the last time.'

'She is your mother.'

'And you are my husband. You're the one who's meant to provide for me.'

'You knew who you were marrying…'

'Did I?' Angry, Sophie turned sharply as if to leave the room and found herself facing a tall dark man standing in the open doorway. He had strong angular features and a mop of unruly hair that framed his attractive face. With a gentle bow he took a step into the room.

'I'm sorry, I hope I'm not interrupting, but I was told that refreshments were available in here. I am Luther Darke.'

Sophie Swailes gave a nervous smile and held out her hand. 'I'm Lady Harcourt's daughter, Sophie, and this is my husband, Gareth.'

With some apparent reluctance, the poet shook Darke's hand also. At that moment Carla entered the room and she and Sophie exchanged hugs and pleasantries.

'You're the artist that my mother has engaged to paint her portrait,' said Sophie, while Carla poured tea for herself and Luther.

'That is correct. I am required to capture the beauty of Lady Harcourt and her Black Pearl. I don't know which will be the greater challenge. True beauty often cannot be captured.'

Sophie seemed at a loss for words at this observation and merely responded with a vague smile. 'I am tired after the journey, Gar. I think I'll have a rest before dinner. If you'll excuse me.'

Darke stared down at the cup of tea that Carla had given him and shuddered. He never drank the stuff. Coffee was the only tolerable hot beverage, and that was usually taken as an accompaniment to brandy.

Carla moved to the window and joined Gareth Swailes to gaze out at the snow-bedecked garden. Now two children had appeared on the scene and were in the process of building a snowman. As they progressed, their darkened figures were almost obliterated from view by the thickening curtain of snow.

'One cannot but think,' said Carla, 'that such dramatic weather provides a fine inspiration for a poet.'

Slowly Swailes turned to Carla and stared at her with unconcealed contempt. 'How would you know?' he said with barely restrained anger, before turning on his heel and leaving the room.

'Charming fellow,' observed Darke as he placed his untouched tea down on a side table. 'We are in for a very affable weekend!' He crossed to join Carla and planted a kiss on the nape of her neck. 'I see we have been beaten to it. Our snowman is almost complete.'

'They have made a splendid job of it. It looks as though it has stepped out of the pages of a storybook.' Darke noted that the snow sculpture now possessed a battered old hat and a carrot nose. The children had fixed a garden broom through one of its arms. One could not help but be charmed by the creation.

'Who are the young spirits? Not guests surely.'

'They are the head gardener's children. Isabel lets them have free rein of the grounds.'

Reaching into his jacket, Darke retrieved a silver flask. 'Watching all that snow chills one. I need some inner fire.' So saying, he took a large gulp from the flask. 'Now that is much more reviving than your unpalatable brown leaves and water.' He grinned as the whisky began its warming process. Outside the children had departed and the solitary snowman stared back at the lighted windows of the great house.

Dinner that night was an ordeal for Luther Darke. He found Isabel Harcourt charming, but the disparate nature of the other guests made conversation around the table stilted and difficult. There were long, uncomfortable silences. To keep himself entertained, Darke viewed the diners as potential sitters and made deductions about their characters. Of Isabel Harcourt's children, he warmed to Sophie more than her elder brother, Randall, whose corpulent waist and shiny red face gave evidence of various overindulgences. When he spoke it was in a boastful manner of some personal triumph on the stock exchange. Darke viewed these claims with some scepticism. There was something about his bluster that persuaded Darke that the gentleman was protesting too much. He felt sure that insecurity, rather than success, was the springboard for such anecdotes.

Although a place had been set for Sebastian Carew, Lady Harcourt's brother, it was empty. 'He must have been delayed by estate business and this snow…' she explained.

Palmer, the jeweller, was a sallow-faced, prim fellow. Certainly ochre would have to be used to capture that flaccid skin and those sunken cheeks. His conversation mainly consisted of flowery compliments, on the food, on the house and, of course, on the Black Pearl. 'I shall be the envy of my fellow craftsmen, being the man to create a frame for such a marvel of nature,' he purred. His speech was as manicured as his nails.

Anthony Cushing, who Darke had secretly awarded the nomenclature 'the amorous neighbour', appeared the most affable of the party. He had a broad fleshy face with small dark, sparkling eyes, sunk deep into their sockets, rosy veined cheeks and a bulbous nose. It would need all of the painter's art to reproduce this face without making it look somehow foolish. In a clumsy and incompetent fashion, he attempted to keep the conversation flowing, addressing each of the diners in turn with queries concerning their health, family and occupations. It was as though he had briefed himself with nuggets of information about each of the guests. He was working hard to impress Lady Harcourt.

'So, Mr Darke,' he said, leaning forward, 'I hear that as well as being an accomplished painter, you are something of a detective.'

'Something of a detective? I could never claim to be that. But I am interested in mysteries, puzzles and as such I have been able to assist Scotland Yard on the odd occasion.'

'Luther is being unusually modest,' observed Carla. 'Without him there would be many unsolved cases in London. Indeed our friend Inspector Thornton regards Luther as his unofficial partner.'

'How exciting,' said Sophie, her features brightening at this titbit of information. She had spoken little during the meal and her puffy eyes bore witness to the fact that she had been crying. 'Perhaps you could tell us about one of your cases.'

Darke cast Carla a reproachful glance. *Now see what you have done.* 'Perhaps tomorrow,' he said gracefully and took a large gulp of red wine to underline that this particular conversational avenue was closed.

It was while the diners were engaged with dessert that Sebastian Carew entered. His mop of greying hair was unruly and damp and his features flushed. 'My apologies to you all. I was caught by the snow on the other side of the estate,' he explained breathlessly as he slumped into the vacant chair at the table. 'Foolishly, I set off on foot this late this afternoon when the snow seemed nothing of a threat. Now it has drifted up to six feet in some places. The road to the village is virtually impassable.' He poured himself a glass of wine and swilled it down in one gulp.

'Does that mean we are trapped here?' asked Palmer, nervously twisting his napkin.

'In a manner of speaking. It has stopped snowing now. In fact it's a beautiful, clear night. But that means freezing temperatures, too, which will harden the layer of snow. It would be a foolish man indeed who attempted a journey tonight, but by noon tomorrow, I'm sure the roads will be passable again.'

'If there is no more snow,' murmured Palmer, almost to himself.

'Well,' said Lady Harcourt cheerily. 'No one is planning to leave until tomorrow afternoon, so let us not worry about the problems until then.'

'Indeed,' cried Carew heartily, pushing his chair away from the table. 'I'll pop off to the kitchen to rescue what food I can, have a quick bath and join you all in the drawing room in half an hour.'

'A good idea,' said Lady Harcourt. 'If the gentlemen would like to remain here for brandy and cigars, I will lead the ladies to the drawing room.'

There were murmurs of agreement to this arrangement.

'Very well. Carla, Sophie and I will leave you gentlemen. Randall, be an angel and fetch that rather special cognac up from the cellar. Carla tells me that Mr Darke is a brandy connoisseur.'

Some ten minutes later, the cognac arrived and Darke poured himself a very large measure. It was an indifferent drink. With some dismay at the promise unfulfilled, Darke stood away from the table, leaning against the fireplace, observing his four companions with the air of a scientist peering down a microscope.

'Tell me, Swailes,' said Randall Harcourt grandly as he swilled his brandy around the glass, his bloated face now perspiring freely, 'is there much money in poetry? I mean, I thought you fellows starved in a garret while scribbling verse.'

'Money is not my god.'

'Maybe not, but you need it to survive. To provide. I sometimes fear for my sister's welfare.'

Swailes' jawline tightened, but with some effort he retained his composure, although Darke noted how firmly clasped his fists were. 'You have nothing to fear on that score, sir. However, if your filial feelings are so strong, perhaps you would like to sponsor my next publication. A mere two hundred pounds should cover the venture.'

It was Randall Harcourt's turn to look uncomfortable. He fidgeted in his chair and mopped his brow before he summoned up a response: 'I only invest in certainties, where my outlay is guaranteed a successful return.'

Anthony Cushing, who had been devouring his cigar with concentrated and obvious pleasure, seemingly oblivious to the undercurrent of animosity flowing between the two men, suddenly pricked up his ears at the mention of the term 'invest in certainties'. 'I say, Randall, if you're able to throw a few hints my way, I would be much obliged. It's been a bad year on the farm and any extra cash to pay the bills would be most welcome. Any whispers on the market of such certainties?'

Randall Harcourt gave a sneer. 'I couldn't possibly reveal anything that would be of any use to you. It is my professional business, and being indiscreet to amateurs would only bring discredit to me.'

'I see,' said Cushing coolly, returning to the pleasure of his cigar.

A cloud of uneasy silence fell upon the company. Palmer rose and pulled back the curtains to look out at the black, cloudless night. He shivered and gave a resigned sigh.

'I think,' said Luther Darke, after swilling the last of his brandy down, 'we should join the ladies.' Oh, he thought, to be back in my own house in town, Carla at my feet, while I stroked her hair; Persephone purring on my lap and the flames of firelight dancing on the large glass of decent brandy at my side.

As soon as Darke entered the drawing room, Isabel Harcourt took him to one side. 'We must devote some time tomorrow for your initial drawings – at your own convenience of course. Forgive me, I am so eager for you to start.' She giggled a girlish giggle that illuminated her face and for an instant banished the wrinkles and signs of care. She was a handsome woman, thought Darke, but twenty years earlier she would have been a rare beauty. He warmed to her enthusiasm and lack of guile.

'I am your servant, ma'am,' he replied, with a mock bow. 'However, if I am not being too presumptuous, I should so like to see this famous trinket of yours which is to feature in the painting.'

'The Black Pearl?'

'The Black Pearl.'

'And so you shall.'

Isabel Harcourt unlocked the bureau, and from one of the small drawers withdrew the grey velvet bag. She turned to face Luther Darke with an almost childish impatience, eager to show off her prize. 'Hold your hand out,' she whispered.

He obeyed and she tipped up the grey bag over his palm. Nothing emerged. With some concern, she pulled the drawstring slacker. Still nothing appeared. Visibly distressed now, her eager fingers scrabbled inside the bag before she gave a cry of despair. 'It's not here. My God, it's not here. It's gone. The Black Pearl has been stolen!'

On making this dramatic discovery, Isabel Harcourt staggered to the chaise longue and slumped down, almost in a faint. Luther Darke rushed to her side and administered whisky from his flask. The drink helped to revive her and she sat up with wild staring eyes. 'We must get the police, Mr Darke. My precious pearl, someone has taken it.'

Darke took her hand and stroked it gently. 'I understand your alarm, but first of all we must be sure the situation is as you perceive it.'

'There can be no doubt about that. The pearl was in my bureau at three-thirty this afternoon; I was showing it to Mr Palmer. And now it is not there. It has been stolen.'

Darke nodded and moved to the bureau. 'Did you lock the bureau before leaving the room?'

Uncertainty clouded Lady Harcourt's features. 'I am … I am not sure. I was so excited about showing it to Mr Palmer and his enthusiasm was so contagious, I may – I suppose – have left it unlocked.'

'Well, there is no sign of a forced entry.'

'How could I have been so foolish? And yet, I suppose I saw no real necessity to lock it away. What threat was there to it?'

Darke knelt at the foot of the bureau and appeared to be examining the carpet.

'You have found something?'

'Nothing of consequence,' he said rising and facing his hostess with a grim expression. 'I am afraid we must face the unpleasant truth of the matter, Lady Harcourt. If the pearl has been taken, stolen, then the thief must be someone in the house. A servant or one of your guests.'

'That is impossible.'

'On the contrary: that is the only possible explanation for its disappearance.'

Lady Harcourt slumped back once more on the chaise longue. 'This is terrible.'

'What do you know of your servants…?'

'Oh, no. There are just John and Marian at the moment. They have been with me for years. I would trust them with my life, let alone the pearl.'

'But presumably you could not say the same about your guests?'

She looked at Darke sharply and paused a moment before replying. 'I am afraid I could not.'

Darke thrust his hands in his pockets and strode to the window, momentarily lost in thought. He gazed out upon the garden below, where the solitary figure of the snowman, bathed in the softened illumination from the house, still stood silently on guard. Darke leaned closer to the glass, staring at the snowman. A faint smile touched his lips.

'One of my guests is a thief. That is the truth of the matter, isn't it, Mr Darke?'

'I am afraid so,' he replied, returning to her side. 'Now, because of the drifting snow, there is no chance of informing the police tonight. It will be daylight before we can attempt to contact them and I'm sure you would like to see this matter cleared up before then. Tonight, in fact.'

'Oh, yes, I would. To be frank with you Mr Darke, the return of my pearl means more to me than apprehending the criminal.'

'I appreciate your sentiment, but the two aspects of the situation are somewhat linked.'

'You think you can solve the matter?'

Darke afforded himself a brief smile. 'I think it is within my powers.'

'How shall you proceed?'

'Obviously the thief will now be aware that you have discovered the pearl's disappearance, and so you must announce that until the police arrive you have given me full powers to investigate the matter and therefore the guests will be obliged to co-operate with my requests. Is that agreeable?'

Lady Harcourt nodded. 'I will do anything to see my pearl returned to me.'

'I shall need to search the bedrooms of each guest. Whoever has taken it will have hidden it. It is unlikely they would keep it about their person.'

'I can let you have a master key to all the bedrooms.'

'Good. That will be my first task. Carla will help me. So then, shall we go down and inform the others?'

There was general dismay and consternation when Isabel Harcourt announced that her precious Black Pearl had been stolen, but these emotions turned to anger and resentment when she explained that she was granting permission to Luther Darke to investigate the matter that evening.

'It pains me to think that someone in this room is responsible for the theft. The loss of my pearl is heartbreaking. It is so precious to me, not because of its worth on the open market, but because of its unmatched beauty and the fact, the very sentimental fact, that it was given to me as a wedding present by Gerald, my late husband.'

'I hope you don't think I'd anything to do with this wretched crime, mother,' snapped Randall. 'It's preposterous.'

'And that goes for Sophie and I. It's a damned insult to be treated like common criminals.' Gareth Swailes' outburst was a signal for a tirade of protests from the others. Lady Isabel silenced them with a raised hand. 'It is a very unfortunate situation, but someone has taken my pearl, someone in this room, and only that person need have any concern or fear regarding Mr Darke's investigation.'

'Isabel's right,' said Sebastian Carew. 'Unconventional though this exercise is, I think it behoves us to go along with it. Only the guilty party has anything to fear. What's your plan of action, Mr Darke?'

'I would ask everyone to stay in this room for the present while Carla and I carry out a search for the pearl.'

'I suppose that means snooping in our rooms, does it?' sneered Gareth Swailes.

'Yes.'

'This is intolerable. I'm leaving at once.'

'I wouldn't advise that, Gareth,' Carew observed, placing a restraining hand on the poet's shoulders. 'It is one sure way of throwing suspicion upon yourself. And besides, you'll get nowhere in the snow tonight. Only a mad man, or a very desperate one, would attempt to leave before the morning.'

Sophie Swailes took her husband's arm and led him to a chair. He sat down mechanically, but his white face was still taut with repressed anger.

'We'll do as we are asked, Mr Darke,' said Sophie.

'I'm happy to co-operate, of course,' affirmed a miserable-looking Walter Palmer.

Anthony Cushing just gave a taciturn nod of agreement and lit up another cigar. His jovial demeanour of an hour ago had clearly dissipated.

Once out in the hallway Luther Darke rubbed his hands with glee. 'This is turning out to be a splendid weekend after all,' he grinned.

'How can you be so callous, Luther? Isabel is distraught about the pearl,' said Carla.

'Oh, she will have the pearl back in her possession before the night is out. Of that I'm sure. But the matter is a splendid conundrum.'

'In what way?'

'It seems to me that with the exception of brother Sebastian, each of our fellow guests has a strong reason for wanting to get his hands on the Black Pearl.'

'Very well, Mr Detective, let's hear your theory that supports this claim.'

'Certainly. When we first arrived I overheard our poet friend, Gareth, urging Sophie to ask her mother for money. I gathered that it wasn't the first time this request had been made and a refusal was a strong possibility. Mr Swailes, it seems, needs money to publish his new book; he even solicited his brother-in-law for funds. That was a foolish request, because it is clear to me that Master Randall is full of bluster and lies. His shabby clothing clearly indicates that he is not half as successful on the stock exchange as he claims. Usually a successful broker does not have a dinner jacket with frayed cuffs.

'Then we come to the would-be suitor. Mr Anthony Cushing has more or less confessed he is in debt; he is faced with "enormous bills" at least. Palmer's admiration for the pearl is unbounded. How he would love it for its own sake, rather than for its market value.'

'You haven't mentioned Sophie or Sebastian.'

'Sophie well might take the pearl for her husband's sake.'

'I can hardly think it. She is such a sweet girl.'

'A sweet girl married to a bully. Who knows what pressures there are in such a marriage.'

'You think Sebastian is without suspicion.'

Darke gave a sardonic grin. 'I did not say that. He is in the same boat as the others, but at present I can discern no obvious motive; but that may well be hidden.'

'If all you say is true, then how are you going to solve the mystery?'

'By searching for further clues. An examination of each of the bedrooms…'

'How will I know what to look for?'

'You won't. If there is something, it will speak to you.'

'Do you think we'll find the pearl in one of the bedrooms?'

'I very much doubt it. I believe I know where the pearl is to be found.'

'What?!'

'The problem at present is not the recovery of that precious dark trinket, but establishing the guilt of the thief. Now let's be about our business. We must not keep our friends waiting too long.'

Darke and Carla worked as a team, examining the five bedrooms in turn. For Carla, it was a very frustrating chore. Nothing appeared to 'speak' to her as Luther had intimated it would.

In Randall Harcourt's chamber, Darke found a third-class return rail ticket to London in his overcoat pocket. 'Further evidence of his penury and lies,' he murmured to himself, replacing the ticket.

Walter Palmer's room was neat and tidy with nothing out of place, but Darke observed in one of the cases an envelope full of newspaper cuttings relating to the Black Pearl.

The Swailes' bedroom, by contrast, was untidy, with cases half-unpacked and clothes flung over the backs of chairs. A manuscript lay on the bedside table bearing the title 'Ferris Awakes'. It was a long narrative poem full of pencilled amendments. Tucked in the pages towards the end was a letter from Hall & Chandler, the publishers, rejecting the work. Darke showed the letter to Carla without comment.

Anthony Cushing's room revealed nothing of the occupant. His case had not been unpacked and there was only his coat hanging behind the door. It was, as Carla observed, as though he had not intended to stay.

Finally they visited Sebastian Carew's bedchamber. Here a fire burned low in the grate, and there was a more comfortable settled air about the room, as was appropriate for one that was used on a permanent basis. Carew's damp overcoat was draped over a chair by the fire. His wet boots had been dumped near the door. 'Strange,' said Darke. 'I would have thought Carew would have placed these by the fire to dry.' He examined them carefully and then turned his attention to some discarded newspapers which he found in the wastepaper basket.

'Well, my love, I hope you are somewhat the wiser for your little investigation,' said Carla as they stood on the landing. 'I am certainly not.'

'I am not wiser, but I am more assured in my suspicions. Before we return to the drawing room, I should like you to see something. Come with me.'

Darke led his companion to Lady Harcourt's study, but instead of showing Carla the bureau from which the pearl had been taken, he took her to the window and drew back the drapes to reveal the snow-covered garden below.

'Take a look at our snowman, my love. Do you notice anything … anything different about him?'

Carla stared for some moments and then said softly, 'The garden broom has gone.'

Darke chuckled. 'Well done. I think it is now time to flush the bird from the covers. Come, let's return to the drawing room.'

On entering the drawing room, Darke was conscious of a tense and angry silence. The occupants had each adopted stiff poses like mannequins, their faces taut and immobile. At his appearance, the figures broke from their frieze-like state and grew animated.

'At last,' cried Gareth Swailes sarcastically. 'The great detective returns. Who have you come to arrest?'

'I don't know whether it's crossed anyone else's mind,' said Randall Harcourt with a sneer as he flopped into an armchair, 'that no one has searched Darke's quarters. He is just as likely to be guilty as anyone else in the house.'

'By Jove, that's a damned good point!' agreed Sebastian Carew with some force.

Lady Harcourt held up her hands in a dramatic gesture. 'Stop it! Stop all this talk. I asked Mr Darke to investigate this matter and I would like to hear what conclusions he has reached, so I would be obliged if you will remain quiet until he has finished.' Her words, calmly but forcefully delivered, had a profound effect on her guests: they immediately resumed their stiff and silent poses, but all eyes were on Luther Darke.

'I will explain the matter, Lady Harcourt, but I cannot change the facts – facts which will, I fear, be painful to you. Your Black Pearl has indeed been stolen by someone in this room, but I am convinced that it was taken on impulse rather than being a planned and calculated robbery. The thief saw various elements fall into place; elements which would assist him not only in the robbery, but also in protecting him from being detected. A house full of guests and the heavy snowfall both played a part in his machinations.'

Darke helped himself to a large glass of brandy and stared at his audience, at their white faces and wide staring eyes. He looked at one face in particular. Was that person hoping, he wondered, praying that I am way off-target in my deductions or was he just counting the moments until he was exposed? He took a large gulp of brandy before resuming.

'A house full of guests, all of whose lives for various reasons would be so much easier if they could get their hands on the kind of wealth that the Black Pearl would realise. Mr Swailes could pay to have his grand opus published and forget about those rejection letters…'

'You devil!' Swailes leapt from his chair, but before he could get any further, Sophie stepped forward and pushed him back down again.

'Shut up, Gareth. Shut up and listen.'

The poet blinked in disbelief at the commanding harshness in his wife's tone. He did as he was bidden.

'Pray continue, Mr Darke,' she said softly.

Darke gave a nod of gratitude. 'A house full of guests … There was Randall, still maintaining the pretence that he was a success on the stock exchange when he in reality he is sinking. I suspect he is sorely in need of money.'

'Not enough to steal from my own mother,' came the bitter response, which Luther Darke ignored.

'Then there is neighbour Anthony Cushing. Mr Carew, as estate manager for your sister, you must have some knowledge of the farming establishments in the neighbourhood.'

'It is part of my duties to be cognisant of such things,' Carew responded.

'And what do you know of the finances of Mr Cushing's farm?'

'I know that due to what I regard as some ill management over the last year, combined with a poor summer, Mr Cushing's business is in some trouble. I would surmise that at present he is sorely in debt.'

'Is that a fairly accurate picture, Mr Cushing?'

The farmer sighed. 'I've been here before and survived, and I'll survive again without the need to steal.'

'Then there is Mr Palmer, a jeweller of great reputation…'

At the mention of his name the little man sat up and shifted to the edge of his chair, his brow moist with perspiration.

'Mr Palmer would value the pearl not for its monetary worth, but as an object of beauty. It would be something to keep hidden and be admired in private moments.'

Palmer did not speak, but shook his head vigorously.

'A house full of guests with possible motives. A suitable smoke-screen to cover up the thief's guilt.'

'Just a moment,' said Cushing. 'If you're listing everyone and their apparent motives for stealing the pearl, what about Sebastian?'

Darke raised an eyebrow. 'Mr Carew, Lady Harcourt's brother: what possible motive could he have for taking the pearl … unless it was to pay off the money lenders for his gambling debts.'

With a sudden cry of anger, Carew rushed at Darke, his arms outstretched. Darke, with practised ease, stepped to the side, allowing his assailant to stumble past him, while at the same time grasping the man's arm from behind. With a nimble twist, he had Sebastian Carew in a tight armlock. 'Nothing is to be gained by violence now, sir. I suggest you sit down and be quiet until I have finished.' So saying, Darke propelled Carew into an empty chair.

Lady Harcourt, her face drained of colour and her eyes bright with wonder, was stunned into silence by the dramatic turn of events.

Darke addressed his assailant in a calm and relaxed manner. 'Your overzealous reaction to my reference to your gambling debts was very timely. It confirmed what I must admit was only a calculated guess. My suspicions were aroused when I found the various pages torn from *The Sporting Life* detailing your bets and the sums of money involved in your wastepaper basket. Bets, it would seem by the number of crosses which far outweighed the ticks, that were unsuccessful.'

'So, I've lost a little money at the track. That doesn't make me a thief.'

'The sums involved were far from little. However, you are quite correct; that alone does not prove that you stole the pearl. Before we go any further, perhaps it would be appropriate for me to restore the pearl to its rightful owner.' He moved to the French window. 'In order to do so, I shall have to go out into the garden.'

So saying, Darke pulled open one of the windows, allowing a cold draught of bitter night air to sweep into the room. As he stepped into the snow-covered garden, the rest of the guests gathered by the window to watch him as he made his way towards the snowman. 'Please note,' he said turning to face his audience, 'the garden broom propped by the wall at the corner of the house and this…' He knelt and picked up a small black object from the snow. 'A piece of coal, not easily seen from downstairs, but clearly visible from the first-floor window. A piece of coal, used by the children for one of the snowman's eyes. It was discarded by the thief when he replaced it with…' Darke paused and, moving to the snowman, removed one of its eyes and held it between his thumb and forefinger. '…The Black Pearl.'

Some minutes later, Luther Darke was back in the sitting room, the French window closed once more and the fire replenished. He stood in the centre of the room with a glass of brandy, holding court.

'I was with Lady Harcourt when she discovered that the pearl was missing. I noticed a damp patch on the floor by the bureau. On examining it, I observed several tiny triangles of snow that had obviously dropped from the thief's boots. Now, Mr Carew was the only person to have been out in the snow in the last few hours, so he became the obvious suspect. On examining his boots in his room, I was able to ascertain that the pattern of the soles matched the triangles of snow I had discovered.

Carew half rose from his chair, about to protest, but Darke silenced him with a wave of his hand. 'I know you didn't take the pearl, but the person who did used your boots to go out into the snow and secrete the pearl in the snowman. A very safe hiding place, indeed. Certainly no one would think to look there. The thief then took the garden broom from the snowman and, walking backwards to the house, swept away his tell-tale footprints. One might think that the pearl could have been stolen any time after Lady Harcourt had shown it to Mr Palmer in the afternoon up to the time the theft was discovered; but if Mr Carew's boots were used to go out into the snow in order to protect the culprit's own shoes, the theft had to take place after Carew had returned to the house and indeed taken his boots off.

'What an inordinate time you were retrieving that brandy, Randall. Not the brandy that had been requested by your mother, was it? You had just grabbed the first bottle that came to hand. That's all you had time for. Why? Because you'd spent the rest of your time stealing the Black Pearl. You'd taken Uncle Sebastian's boots from his room while he was bathing, and gone into the garden to secrete the pearl in the snowman. Then, with time running out, you returned the boots, just flinging them back in Carew's room rather than replacing them by the fire. But when you returned to the dining room, sweating more than usual, I noticed that the bottoms of your trousers were somewhat damp. Rather like mine are now. The snow out there is quite deep – deep enough to creep over a pair of boots.'

'It's a lie.' Randall spoke without conviction, his fat, shiny face drained of colour.

'No, sir, the lie is that you are a successful stockbroker. The truth is that you need money desperately, and yet you are too arrogant to ask for assistance from your mother. You prefer to steal, rather than admit the truth.'

'Randall, is all this true?' said Lady Harcourt with a mixture of disbelief and horror.

Her son's response was to throw his head in his hands and commence sobbing.

'Well, that was a far better weekend than I had anticipated,' observed Luther Darke, as the carriage rattled through the gateway of Barrington Hall. It was early afternoon the following day, and already the feverish yellow sun had melted the snow sufficiently to allow the carriage easy access onto the open road.

'I don't know how you can say that,' said Carla. 'It has been quite distressing for Isabel. To learn that she cannot trust her own son.'

'Even the darkest of shadows harbours some light. Some good will come of this matter, I am sure. It is an incident that will bring mother and son closer together. Randall no longer has the pressures of the pretence that he created in order to find acceptance. They can both be more honest with each other now. The fact that Lady Harcourt intends to take no action against her son will help to create a stronger bond between them. He has learned a useful lesson before it is too late.'

'I believe you could be right.'

'I am always right.'

Carla pulled a long face and gave Darke a friendly dig in the ribs. 'I must admit, your detective work was very impressive. The way you worked out where the pearl was hidden was quite brilliant.'

Darke's eyes twinkled, delighted by Carla's praise. 'The clues were there, fragile as they were; but I must confess that I had to make some leaps of imagination, too. Randall's hiding place was ingenious. The house could have been swarming with the police turning everything upside down, but no one would think of looking at the innocent snowman in the garden, staring into the house with its two dark eyes.'

'Except you, my darling, except you,' said Carla, kissing him on the cheek.

Luther Darke sat back in the carriage and grinned broadly.

4

THE RIDDLE OF
THE VISITING ANGEL

Who would have thought of it? he mused. Out of science came ethereal mysticism that paved the way to fortune. He smiled a self-satisfied smile. *No one* would have thought of it – except himself.

Cornelius Horden sat up in bed, clasping a silver-framed photograph of his wife. His eyes misted as he gazed at the faded image, one which had been captured over twenty years before. To Cornelius, who loved his wife with an unstinting passion, she had never changed from the fresh, graceful young woman she had been in that long-lost summer in the late 1870s. He had never perceived her golden hair turning to grey or the smoothness of her skin slacken and give way to wrinkles. For him, her beauty remained intact – remained so until death. While Gwendolyn's ageing never impinged upon his consciousness, her passing now consumed him. He knew that to commit suicide would be against his own strict personal moral code, and so he found himself enduring a desolate and achingly sad existence. Gently he brought his lips to touch the cold glass of the photograph frame. 'Oh, Gwen,' he murmured softly, as the tears began to flow with unabandoned grief. Only his noble sensibilities prevented him from taking his own life.

Moments later, he recovered sufficiently to place the photograph on the bedside table and wipe his eyes with one of his wife's handkerchiefs. He gave a deep melancholic sigh that seemed to suck the energy from his tired frame.

There came a gentle knock at the bedroom door and a young woman entered. In some ways she was like a younger, harsher image from the photograph, but her hair was dark and worn in a severe style, pulled back from the face. By comparison, her features were pinched and shrewish. She lacked the grace or charm of her mother.

'I wondered if you'd like a hot drink, Father.'

He shook his head.

She noticed his red eyes and tear stained cheeks. Her glance fell upon the photograph. The old man read his daughter's mind. 'I've been saying goodnight to your mother. I'm ready to sleep now, Sarah.'

'Very well, Father.' She came forward and planted a chaste kiss on his forehead. 'Shall I pull the curtains? There's a full moon tonight. I'm sure the light will bother you.'

'No, no,' said the old man with an irrational urgency. 'If I wake, I like to see the world outside … the sky. With the curtains drawn, my world is so … so claustrophobic.'

Sarah said nothing. Since her mother's death, six months before, her father's grief had led him into strange ways and he had developed odd little behaviours. It had isolated him from the rest of the family so that now he was almost a stranger to them. It was as though he had deliberately cut himself off from all those who cared for him in order to live in a world of sadness and memories.

'If there is nothing else, I'll leave you.'

'There's nothing else.'

'Goodnight, Father.'

'Goodnight.'

Sarah swished from the room, closing the door noisily.

Cornelius gave a sigh of relief. He was alone again with Gwendolyn. He closed his eyes and soon shallow sleep overtook him.

He woke again some twenty minutes later. He was immediately conscious of a soft sound invading the room. He lay in the darkness, listening intently. He thought he heard someone calling his name, softly, persuasively. He sat upright, straining to determine exactly the nature of this sound. Surely it was not a voice. It must be just his imagination? The air was still and quiet … and yet…

He glanced at the photograph on the bedside table, the moonlight highlighting the ghostly faded features of his dead wife. Was the smile more vibrant and were the eyes sunnier? Did the lips appear to move? Cornelius Horden closed his eyes apprehensively.

And then he heard the voice once more – clearly this time. There could be no doubt. It was calling his name, softly but distinctly. The tone was high, but he was not sure whether it was a man or a woman's voice. He struggled into an upright position and only then allowed himself to open his eyes. What he saw made him catch his breath in such a violent fashion that he thought for a moment that he would faint.

There, against the darkness of the windowpane was a flickering, bright light that gradually formed itself into an image. It was the image of an angel. Or a creature that he recognised as an angel from the illustrations of the scriptures he'd seen as a child. A tall figure with flowing blonde hair, dressed in a long white gown behind which two large dove-like wings were visible. They flapped slowly and noiselessly. The beautiful epicene face of the creature was topped with a shining halo. It was an angel, indeed. One of God's holy messengers, who had come to him. The angel was smiling, its arms stretched out in a beckoning gesture, beckoning for Cornelius to join him.

The vision warmed the old man's tired, grieving heart. Instinctively, he sat forward in the bed and reached out, his fingers stretching in the darkness towards the shimmering figure. And then as quickly and as suddenly as the apparition had appeared, it vanished. The blue of the night seeped back to replace it. The room regained its shadows.

Cornelius sat for some time staring at that bleak space, barely moving a muscle. His tired brain tried to rationalise his experience. It couldn't. He knew he hadn't been asleep; he hadn't been dreaming, and he hadn't imagined it. There was only one lucid explanation left.

He had been visited by an angel.

But why?

'Have you ever heard of the Church of the True Resurrection?'

'I have not, but it sounds like so many of the crank religious organisations we encounter in London nowadays, run by the weak-minded for the weak-minded.'

Luther Darke stared at his friend Inspector Edward Thornton with some surprise. 'How harshly cynical of you. Police work is brutalising your sensitivities.'

'I am not a religious man, Luther, although I hope I am a moral one in keeping with the Christian tradition. But I have no time for the mumbo-jumbo that some of these so-called holy sects indulge in. They befuddle the minds of the gullible – invariably for profit.'

The two men were seated by the fireside in the sitting room of Darke's town house in Manchester Square. A pale noonday sun sent frail yellow shafts of light into the otherwise gloomy chamber. Luther Darke liked the gloom.

He took another drink of whisky. 'Do you know of a fellow by the name of Doctor Sebastien Le Page?'

Thornton screwed his face up in a pantomime of thought.

Darke grinned. 'Oh, Edward, Edward, you are being singularly useless.'

'Has Mr Le Page committed a crime?'

'Doctor, please. Do give the scoundrel his proper title. Committed a crime? Ah, well there is the rub, my dear friend. One cannot be absolutely sure. However, I am fairly certain he is in the process of doing so.'

'Riddles again, Luther.'

'Always riddles. Of course. Life would be meaningless without them.'

Thornton slipped his watch from his waistcoat. 'I have to be at the Yard in an hour, so I would appreciate it if we could deal with practicalities.'

Darke gave a throaty laugh. 'Ever the professional when the smell of crime is in the air. But I have to say, Edward, that I am disappointed. I'm not sure whether it is with you for never having heard a wrong word against Doctor Charlatan Le Page, or because the aforementioned knave has managed to keep his nefarious dealings out of the purview of Scotland Yard and its eagle-eyed officers.'

'It is an unusual name. French, I assume. Perhaps we know him under an alias. However, you invited me here for a drink and an intriguing story. Well, I've been furnished with a drink.' He held up a full tumbler of whisky. 'So now let me have your story, and then maybe I can say more about Doctor Le Page.'

Darke did not reply instantly, but stared at the dancing flames in the grate for some moments before addressing his friend in a quiet and sober manner. 'Tell me, Edward, do you believe in angels?'

Thornton failed to hide the surprise that this query brought. 'Angels?'

'Those celestial and divine messengers – possessors of halos and large white wings. You remember that one of their breed appeared before the shepherds tending their sheep outside Bethlehem the night Jesus Christ was born. Do you believe in them?'

Despite the irreverence of this utterance, Thornton knew that Darke was not jesting. The inspector shook his head. 'I must admit I have never given it any thought. I think I would need to see one before I could pass judgement.'

With a sigh of satisfaction, Luther Darke leaned back in his chair, both hands cradling his whisky glass. 'It is possible that could be arranged.'

The policeman looked shocked.

Darke smiled. 'Let me tell you my story.'

The day following the angel's visitation, Cornelius Hordern was in a notably more cheerful mood than usual. And this was in spite of the fact that Sarah had pestered him to have stern words with Sadie, the youngest housemaid, whose courting habits were causing her to be out late in the evenings of her days off, with the result that she was sullen and lethargic in the mornings.

'She is young, my dear. Do not deny the girl her youth,' he said gently, pulling his chair closer to the fire.

'We must not indulge these girls, Father. Give them an inch … you know as well as I that I am a supporter of women's rights. But if women are to be taken seriously, they must respect their responsibilities and not shirk them in favour of a kiss and a cuddle with one of the village lads.'

Cornelius Hordern gazed at his daughter. How unlike her mother she was. Despite a passing resemblance in looks, the brusqueness of her demeanour and the lack of generosity of spirit destroyed any true filial resemblance. 'I will speak to her,' said Hordern with resignation.

As it turned out, some hours later Sadie tapped on the old man's study door and announced that he had a visitor. 'Johnson has taken Miss Sarah into the village on a shopping expedition, sir, and it's Clara's day off. It was left up to me to answer the door, and there's a gentlemen who says he is here on urgent business.' The words tumbled out in an excited gasp, her animated face alive with emotion. Cornelius could not help but smile at this lively, natural creature. This was the girl with whom he was meant to remonstrate. Certainly here was no sulleness or lethargy.

He smiled at her. 'What does this gentleman want, Sadie?'

'He didn't say, but said I was to give you his card.' She thrust an ivory visiting card into her master's hand.

Cornelius gazed at it. It bore the owner's name and address in bold black print: 'Doctor Sebastien Le Page, 13 Plover Mansions, Highgate, London', and underneath, scrawled in pencil, the word 'angel'. Cornelius Hordern felt his heart miss a beat.

'You'd better show the gentleman in,' he said, at length.

Sebastien Le Page was a short, dapper man, with swarthy features, thinning black hair and a neatly trimmed moustache. Two large eyes peered out at the world through a carefully balanced pince-nez. He strode purposefully into the room and grasped Cornelius Hordern's hand with a tight, icy grip.

'I thank you most profusely for seeing me, sir,' he said easily. The voice held a faint trace of a French accent.

Hordern waved his visitor to a chair but did not reply until Sadie had left the room. 'I would appreciate it if you could come straight to the point and explain the purpose of your visit.'

Theatrically, Le Page attempted to hide a secret smile. 'Cards on the table, eh? So sensible, I agree. Very well. I will not prevaricate. The matter is too important to be hindered by formal niceties. Last night you experienced a wondrous event. You were visited by a spiritual messenger.'

Hordern found his mouth going dry and he could hardly summon the words in response. 'How on earth can you possibly know that?'

A self-satisfied smile lighted upon Le Page's face. 'Because it is my business ... my calling to know such things. I am high priest of the Church of the True Resurrection.'

Hordern shook his head. 'That means nothing to me.'

'Our disciples believe in a life beyond this life: a life of peace and harmony. An existence that allows communication between the two worlds.'

Hordern curled his lip. 'You mean Spiritualists?'

'Our movement is a branch of Theosophy, yes, but our faith in the interaction of physical and ethereal agents is greater and more assured.'

'I don't wish to be rude, sir, but I have little time or belief...'

Le Page leaned forward and lowered his voice. 'Your wife has been speaking to me.'

These words sent involuntary icy shudders through Hordern's body. He shook his head in disbelief and yet he desired to hear more.

'She is happy and wishes to communicate with you. That is why the angel came last night, as I knew it would, to bring you to her.'

'This is outrageous, Doctor Le Page, you are playing with my emotions. My beloved wife is dead and now beyond my reach.'

'You deny the existence of your eyes?'

'I saw nothing. I was dreaming.' The old man shook his head in some distress and ran his bony fingers across his brow. 'Please, I beg you to go and leave me now. Leave me this instant.'

Le Page did not seem at all perturbed by his curt dismissal. He rose calmly and walked to the door. 'Should you change your mind, Mr Hordern, you have my card. Good day.'

That night Cornelius Hordern lay awake in his bed, propped up on pillows, staring at the window opposite. He fought against sleep overtaking him. He wished to watch all night to see if the angel came again.

However, as the church clock in the distance chimed two o'clock, he began to lose his battle against drowsiness. His eyelids drooped and he slipped down under the covers into the warmth of the bed. Gradually he grew aware of the irrationality of the situation. What on earth was he doing? This whole business was all nonsense. The explanation was simple: he had dreamed up the angel. His grief had somehow stimulated his imagination and…

Suddenly, he heard his name. A faint, thin voice calling softly on the air. It was repeated three times.

'Yes,' he found himself replying to the darkness.

Almost on the instant he spoke, a light filtered into the room. The angel had appeared once more, exactly as it had done the previous night. It was a shimmering image seen through the darkened pane of the window, its arms spread wide in an act of supplication.

'Sarah!' Cornelius Hordern yelled. 'Sarah, for God's sake, come here!' He pulled back the covers, stumbled from the bed and called out his daughter's name again, his eyes never leaving the flickering vision.

Within seconds, Sarah burst into her father's bedroom, a dressing gown hastily pulled around her thick calico nightgown.

'What is it, Father?' she cried. 'Are you ill?'

'Look,' he said, pointing at the window.

Bewildered, the young woman did as her father instructed and then gave a gasp of terror, for she too saw the visiting angel.

And then in an instant the apparition disappeared, vanished into the blackness of the night.

'Now I am intrigued,' said Inspector Edward Thornton taking a sip of whisky.

Darke's face creased into a smile. 'I thought you might be. When the father and daughter had regained their composure, they gazed out of the window into the garden, but there was no sign of anything unusual. The angel, the celestial visitor, call it what you will, had left no trace. However, now his daughter had seen it, Cornelius Hordern was convinced of its existence.'

Plover Mansions was a smart address and number 13 was the large penthouse apartment at the top of this modern building. A young, tall, dark-haired man wearing a short beard and dressed from head to foot in black showed Cornelius Hordern into Sebastien Le Page's study.

Le Page looked up from his desk and gave his visitor a self-satisfied smile. 'Take a seat, Monsieur Hordern. I felt sure that we should meet again. Perhaps not as soon as this, but here you are. And … now you believe.'

Hordern nodded dumbly.

'Excellent. Now it becomes possible for us to help each other.'

'Tell me, Luther, how did you get mixed up in this business?'

'Indirectly – as always. It was Carla who first told me of the affair. She knows Sarah Hordern through a women's discussion group they both belong to. One night after a meeting, Miss Hordern sought out Carla for advice. My darling Carla, being the kind soul she is, whisked the creature off to her own apartment in Bloomsbury so that she could unburden her soul or whatever was necessary…'

'My brother is away in America on business and I've no one else to turn to for advice. I feel stupid for being so weak but…' Sarah Hordern's lip trembled and for a few moments Carla thought she was going to burst into tears.

'It's a weakness to bottle things up inside you, Sarah. Tell me everything you wish and I will help if it's possible.'

'Thank you. The whole situation is a crazy one. My father is giving away the family fortune to a crank medium. Before long we shan't have a home to live in.'

'You realise, Monsieur Hordern, that I do not usually carry out a séance with only one disciple present, but thanks to your extremely generous contribution to the coffers of the Church of the True Resurrection, I am more than happy to make an exception.'

'It is I who cannot thank you enough.'

'We are both satisfied then. Well, if you are ready, let us go through to my communication chamber.'

Le Page led his new disciple into a small room off his study. The chamber was lined with black velvet curtains. A round table stood in the centre of the room upon which was placed a single candlestick, the solitary, erratic flame the only source of illumination.

'Sit on my right,' said Le Page taking the most ornate chair. 'Place your hands on the table. It is essential that they remain there throughout the whole course of the séance. Is that understood?'

Cornelius nodded.

'You must prepare yourself mentally for what is about to happen. It is most likely that your wife will speak to you – in some form – tonight. After all she did send an angel to bring you to me, but you must not be too disappointed if very little happens on this occasion. Just as this is a strange and daunting experience for you, so it will be for your wife. You can only expect to build up trust over a period of time.'

Cornelius was so emotionally strained at this point that he could barely respond with a nod. The thought of being able to communicate with his beloved Gwendolyn again was almost too much for his weary constitution to bear. He sat quietly in a frozen state of anticipation.

Le Page flicked him a quick smile. 'Very well, let us begin. First of all clear your head of all thoughts except for the image of your wife, Gwendolyn. Fix her face firmly in your mind.'

Hordern did as he was bidden.

Le Page sat back in the chair. He remained still for some moments, breathing deeply with his eyes closed. Then with a sudden movement, he flung his head back as though he were addressing the ceiling and he began talking in a strange strangulated whisper. 'Listen to our plea, oh silent spirits of the other world. We are believers, longing to reach out through the invisible barrier that separates the flesh from the soul to send our love to you. Let us speak with you, oh spirits. We are your devout believers. Speak to us.'

The candle flame flickered and went out.

There was silence for a moment and then Le Page repeated his plea: 'Speak to us.'

'Who is it who calls to us?' The voice was strange, muffled and indistinct, and, to Hordern's heightened senses, it seemed to be emanating from the ceiling.

'We have a sad earthbound soul here who wishes to speak to a loved one who has passed through the veil. Our friend is Cornelius Hordern.'

The strange voice came again. 'What is it he wishes to ask?'

'Speak. Ask,' prompted Le Page, squeezing Hordern's arm.

For some time, Cornelius Hordern could not utter a word. Now he had arrived at this longed-for moment, his brain was not able to function. The fear of disappointment was crippling his faculties.

'You must speak. She will not respond to me,' said Le Page in an urgent whisper.

With trembling tones, Hordern addressed the darkness. 'Gwendolyn, my darling, are you there?'

There was a moment's pause and then a rustling sound came to his ears. 'Gwendolyn,' he asked with greater urgency. And then he froze, for on the air he smelt the faint traces of perfume wafting around him. It was his wife's favourite fragrance. As his racing brain was trying to assimilate this sensation, there came another voice.

'Darling, darling Cornelius.'

It was Gwendolyn. It must be.

'My dear,' Hordern sobbed, his hands momentarily raised from the surface of the table as though he was going to reach out and embrace his dead wife.

'Oh, Cornelius, do not fear. I am happy, my darling, and I will wait for you.'

'Can't … can't I see you?'

'Come again,' replied the voice as it trailed away to silence.

'Gwendolyn!' Hordern cried, tears now falling down his cheeks.

But there was no reply.

'You have been lucky, my dear sir. Very lucky indeed.' It was Le Page who was talking, in his normal voice. 'That was a remarkable contact for the first time. Remarkable.'

In the darkness Cornelius Hordern sought out the medium's hands and wrung them with gratitude. 'It was a miracle. My darling Gwen so near. How can I ever repay you?'

'Since that first séance, there have been three more. Each time, my father has made huge donations to this so-called Church of the True Resurrection. He cannot see that this Le Page is a charlatan.'

'Are you sure?' asked Carla, in all seriousness.

Sarah Hordern looked shocked. 'I have no doubt in my own mind.'

'Despite the fact that you witnessed the visiting angel?'

'Well, it is true that I cannot explain what I saw, but I am convinced that my father is being tricked in the most treacherous fashion.'

'I think you should meet a friend of mine. He is very good at explaining the inexplicable.'

Luther Darke listened to the whole story without interruption. He sat with his eyes closed, stroking his cat, Persephone, who lay upon his lap. When Sarah Hordern had finished her narrative, he sat thoughtfully for a moment and then suddenly jumped from his chair, an action that sent the slumbering cat spinning into the air. With muttered apologies to Persephone as she landed in an undignified fashion on the rug by the fire, Darke rushed to the bookcase.

'Just let me check something out, Miss Hordern, and then I will attend to your little problem,' he said, poring over one of his own commonplace volumes. 'Ah, here we have it. I thought the name was lodged somewhere in the great cluttered attic of this brain of mine. What detritus I do collect there.'

With a satisfied grin, he returned to his seat.

'What name do you mean? Sebastian Le Page? Do you know him?'

Darke waved his hand casually. 'Not personally. We shall come to that later. First of all, let me deal with the séances. From what you have told me these are simple, amateur affairs. Your father has never actually seen your mother at one of these shows?'

Sarah Hordern shook her head. 'According to what he told me, the nearest he came to that was a shadowy female figure wearing a dress similar to the type my mother wore.'

'Well, all these little tricks can be accounted for quite easily. Dim lighting in a dark room with drapes on the walls allows for a number of accomplices to create numerous tricks. The perfume that your mother wore, for example, would be sprayed near your father at the appropriate moment. A muffled female voice which says little and yet professes to be your mother can be most convincing in such circumstances, especially when your father wants to believe it is her in the first place. So, we can eliminate any special magic in the séances. It is the angel that is the masterstroke. It is the appearance of this celestial visitor that has fully convinced your father that such supernatural shenanigans are possible; and thus gives credence to these medium shows. Therefore, it is this winged messenger that is to be the focus of our investigation.'

'What are you going to do?'

'First I should like to come down to your house and scrutinise the scene of the visitation. I would need a couple of hours for such an investigation when your father was not there. Is that possible?'

'He comes up to town every Friday to lunch with an old friend and play billiards at his club. He leaves on the ten o'clock train and returns at six.'

'Excellent. Would a visit this Friday be acceptable to you?'

'And so, my dear Inspector Thornton, I thought you would like to accompany me on my little investigation down at the Hordern residence. It is situated near Leatherhead.'

'How can I resist? You have made the whole affair sound quite intriguing.'

'Well, I suspect it will be instructional. Along the way we should learn how to create an angel.'

The Hordern house, a three-storey mock Gothic pile built in the 1840s, was situated some three miles from Leatherhead. The two friends engaged the services of a dogcart to deliver them to the doorstep. As this vehicle rattled up the driveway, Edward Thornton put a question to Luther Darke, one which he had been on the verge of asking ever since he first had been told of this affair. He had assumed – wrongly – that Darke would provide the answer without being prompted. Thornton now saw that this wasn't to be the case.

'Tell me,' he said as casually as he could, 'what is there about the name Sebastien Le Page? You have heard it before?'

Darke grinned. 'What patience you have. I have been waiting hours, days for you to question me on that. Your restraint is admirable. Yes, I have heard it before. In a completely different context.'

Thornton waited a moment, but Darke was playing games and said nothing.

'What context?'

'Do you remember – it was in the summer of 1896 – the stir the Lumière brothers made in London with their cinematography exhibition?'

Thornton shook his head. 'I do not recall it.'

'It was a wonderful show. I went twice. It was so entertaining to watch the audience grow nervous during the showing of 'L'Arrivée d'un Train'. They really believed that a locomotive was steaming towards them in the little theatre.'

'What has this to do with Sebastien Le Page?'

'I still have the programme from the event. For some reason the name of the projectionist lodged in a corner of my mind. It was Sebastien Le Page.'

On arriving at the house, Darke asked to see Cornelius Hordern's bedroom. He was not surprised to learn that it was on the ground floor.

'This is not a new arrangement; my parents have always slept down here. I think it may have been as a result of their stay in India when they lived in a bungalow. Since my mother died, I moved into the room next door to be near my father in the night if he needed me.'

'As he did the other evening when you too were able to witness the angel,' observed Thornton.

The young woman nodded.

To Thornton's surprise, his friend's examination of the room seemed cursory and brief. 'Only one item of interest there,' Darke whispered as they left the room. 'The speaking tube.'

Leaving Sarah Hordern in the house to arrange refreshments, the two men then investigated the grounds, and in particular, the area outside Cornelius Hordern's bedroom. Close to the shrubbery, about twenty yards from the bedroom window, Thornton discovered some marks in the wet earth.

'Good man,' cried Luther Darke, bending down to examine them. 'Two sets of footprints – one fellow wearing heavily ribbed boots. And look here: three round indentations, each about two feet apart in a triangular arrangement.' Suddenly he burst out laughing. 'That clinches it, my dear Edward. We have caught our angel.'

'Before we leave,' said Darke some twenty minutes later as he and Thornton sat with Sarah Hordern in the drawing room, 'I should very much like to have a word with your flirtatious maid, Sadie.'

Miss Hordern looked surprised. 'If you wish. But I don't quite…'

'It's just to settle a few points in my mind.'

'Very well, I'll send for her now.'

'And, Miss Hordern, I think it would be best if we saw her alone.'

'If that is what you wish.' A certain frostiness had crept into the woman's voice now.

'She will feel more at ease if her employer is not standing in the background, and therefore it will be easier for us to get at the truth,' explained Thornton.

The maid arrived promptly and, with some reluctance, her mistress left her with the two investigators.

Darke smiled at the pretty young girl. 'First of all, Sadie, you are not in trouble, and anything you say to me will not be repeated to your master or your mistress. It is just that my friend and I are trying to clear up a little mystery that is puzzling Miss Sarah, and I think you can help us.'

'Help you? I don't know anything.'

'Now, how can you be sure of that until I've asked you a few questions? Eh?'

The girl looked sullenly to the floor. 'I don't know, sir.'

'Now then, it is true to say that in the past Miss Sarah has reprimanded you for lateness in the morning...'

'Not recently, sir.'

'Good. No more suitors, then?'

'Well...'

'Something a little more permanent, I see by the silver ring on your hand.'

Instinctively, the girl covered up the ring with her right hand. 'It's just a present.'

'From whom?'

'From a friend.'

'From your young man?'

'Yes, sir.'

'Not a local lad, is he?'

Again the maid hesitated.

'Come, come, Sadie, the truth will out.'

'No, he's not local. He's better than the layabouts and ruffians that live round here.'

'He must be. That ring is quite fine.'

'He's a good man, sir, and ... I love him.'

'Tall, thin, dark-haired with a short beard?'

'You know him?'

'That will be all now, Sadie. You may return to your duties.'

After the maid had left, Darke shook his head sadly. 'What is it the bard says in *Macbeth*? "but in this house I keep a servant fee'd." Ah, well. Time to return to London, Edward. On the train, we shall plan our campaign of action and discuss two letters that we must write.'

Dear Cornelius,

Due to circumstances beyond my control, I have to leave London for a week on pressing business, and therefore I shall have to cancel our Wednesday appointment. I know how upset this will make you feel, but I assure you my trip is essential. However I shall be back in London on the twenty-first of this month and hope to see you on that date.

Yours sincerely,

Sebastien

Dear Dr Le Page,

I have decided to cease my connection with The Church of the True Resurrection. My recent experiences have been most unsatisfactory and I now begin to wonder if the divine intervention, which I witnessed at the start of our association, was in fact an illusion – a dream perhaps.

Therefore I shall be making no further contributions to the funds of your organisation. In order to help me overcome my recent disappointments, I intend to take a protracted trip abroad and I leave in two days' time on the fourteenth of this month.

Yours sincerely,

Cornelius Hordern

It was past midnight and Cornelius Hordern was still awake. Despite the lateness of the hour, he did not feel drowsy at all. He was sitting up in bed, waiting for the night to pass. The sudden cancellation of his weekly séance at Le Page's apartment had upset him terribly. He had come to live for those few sweet moments when, albeit in an insubstantial fashion, he was reunited with Gwendolyn. The snatches of speech, the breath of her perfume, were wondrous to him. He hadn't quite realised how much he had come to depend upon the séances until this cancellation. There would be next week, of course, but that was six long agonising days away.

He sighed heavily and stared out at the blue blankness of the night sky. There was at least one comforting aspect of this affair: his gradual realisation that he had misjudged his daughter. In the last few weeks, as his own pain had lessened, he had begun to view Sarah in a different light. He could see now that in her own way she cared for him very deeply, and it was unfair of him to compare the girl to her mother. Both were unique and of a different time. For him no one could match Gwendolyn's sweetness and beauty, but now he saw that Sarah had her own individual fire. She was a good daughter, and what she lacked in warmth, she made up for in decency and care. He resolved to be kinder to her in the future. This resolution eased his mind a little. Perhaps he should now try to get some sleep.

Just as he was about to slip down under the covers, a sound came to his ears. It was the sound that he had heard before. His name was called, softly, wistfully in the gloom of the bedroom. It came again: louder, more insistent, demanding a response. It resonated in his tired brain.

'Yes, I am here,' he said. 'I am here.'

As though this utterance was a cue, no sooner had he replied to the disembodied voice than a light shone into the bedroom through the window. Caught in the dancing ray was the figure of an angel. It appeared exactly as it had done before; even the actions of supplication were identical.

Why had it come again? What was the purpose of its visitation this time? Confused and distressed, Cornelius Hordern called out to his daughter. With remarkable alacrity, the girl came into the room and rushed to his side.

'It's the angel,' he muttered, shaking his head in confusion. 'Why has it come again?'

'Don't worry, Father. There's nothing to be concerned about now.' As she spoke, the image of the angel wavered and slid upwards towards the ceiling of the room before disappearing altogether. Without a word, Sarah Hordern led her father to the window. They looked out into the moonlit garden beyond, where they heard voices raised in anger. Dimly, they saw a group of men, one of whom appeared to be a uniformed policeman.

Sarah gasped with delight. 'They've captured your angel,' she said.

One of the men turned his face towards them. It was white and contorted in anger. It belonged to Doctor Sebastien Le Page.

Dawn was breaking and pink light was seeping into the sky when Cornelius Hordern, now dressed in his day clothes, and his daughter sat together in the drawing room with two men.

'It's time I introduced you to Mr Luther Darke and Inspector Edward Thornton,' she announced, passing her father a cup of hot tea. She and Thornton also had cups of the reviving brew but, as usual, Darke had requested free rein with the brandy decanter.

Hordern looked pale and bewildered. 'I wish you would tell me exactly what has been going on, Sarah. What was Doctor Le Page doing here? I thought he was out of the country. And why are the police involved?'

'You must forgive me, father, for going behind your back as I did, but I acted for your own good. I felt in my heart that this angel business was all wrong. It was just instinct, I know, but I just knew that something was not quite right. And when you started giving your fortune away to Le Page...' The girl began to cry.

'But, Sarah, you were looking for rationalities in the world of the spiritual. Doctor Le Page is...'

'A fraud, sir,' said Darke finishing his sentence. 'In some state of distress, your daughter asked me to investigate Le Page and "this angel business". I suspect that if I had told her that the good old Doctor was Moses reborn and that he had a cupboard full of the heavenly host, she would have accepted the situation and been pleased for you. She just wanted things to be right and proper for her father, and an independent investigation would present the truth – or as near the truth as we ever get to in this life.'

'I see,' said Hordern quietly. 'And what is the truth?'

'The truth is that Sebastien Le Page is running the most genteel of extortion rackets. He discovers rich widows or widowers, and then arranges for the angel to pay a nightly visit. This is followed up with a personal call from the man himself. As he did with you.'

'As he did with me,' repeated Hordern dully. 'But what about the angel?'

'I'll come to that later, sir. First, let me run through the extortion process. I suspect your reaction to Le Page's first visit was a fairly standard one. Le Page would be used to and prepared for the initial rejection. But another nightly vision and the bereaved victim is hooked, convinced that the angel brings greetings from beyond the grave. That was the really clever part of the scheme. If you believe that a heavenly visitor is prompting this spiritual communion, you are more likely to accept the various fairground theatricals that follow. There are numerous fake mediums in London, but none with such prestigious credentials as one with an angel on his side.'

'You mean all those séances were … were false. I didn't communicate with my dear wife?' The old man's voice trembled with emotion as he sought confirmation from his daughter.

She shook her head.

'Everything you experienced in the dark during those sessions can be explained away as a trick.' It was Edward Thornton who spoke now. 'There would be an accomplice, maybe more than one, in the room with you. They would be dressed in black from head to foot so you could not see them. In this way candles can be blown out, perfume sprayed in the air, material rustled as though a woman is present and even a vague shape may be glimpsed. Any female voice in such a situation could be easily accepted as the one that your heart desires it to be.'

Hordern, his eyes now moist with tears, ran his fingers through his hair. 'I've been a fool. A gullible old fool.'

'You have been a victim, Mr Hordern. One of many, I am sorry to say. Once you were ensnared, then Le Page could ask you for money, large amounts of money, and you were grateful to pass it over to him. As Luther observed, it is the most genteel form of blackmail.'

'But how did Le Page manage the angel illusion?'

'Aha,' said Luther rubbing his hands, 'that is where our Mr Le Page – the Doctor qualification is also false – was exceedingly clever. He was at one time principal projectionist to the Lumière brothers in their cinematography show – moving pictures. No doubt while working with them he had the idea for the angel illusion. You photograph an actor who is dressed as an angel against a black background with a moving picture camera. All you need is about ninety seconds of film. And then you project the film against a window at night, using it as a transparent screen. The image can be seen on the other side, as though the angel is real and suspended in mid-air.'

'This is incredible,' said Cornelius Hordern shaking his head in wonder.

'Ingenious, I would say, but not incredible. In fact, sir, it is far more credible than the alternative. The inspector and I found signs in the grounds near your bedroom window where the tripod supporting the projector had rested for the celestial film show. As for the voice in your bedroom calling your name, you need look no further than your maid, Sadie. I am afraid she was seduced into assisting in this charade by one of Le Page's handsome accomplices. No doubt he promised wealth and marriage and, silly little girl that she is, she fell in with their plans. She used the speaking tube in your bedroom as a means of creating the disembodied voice. On the night of the visitation, she would ensure that the stopper on the tube in your room was removed and at the appointed time she would call your name through the tube from the kitchen. It was an essential part of the plan. The projectionist had to be sure you were awake before he began to run the film. No doubt it was Sadie who took some of your wife's perfume for Le Page to use.'

'The iniquitous girl!' cried Hordern.

'Do not be too hard on her. What she did, she did for love or affection and we all know what fools that powerful emotion can make of us.'

Hordern's face broke into a wry grin. 'How right you are, Mr Darke.' He leaned forward and held his arms out to his daughter. She slipped easily into his embrace. 'I think that my acquaintance with the angels has done me the world of good. I have learned that while I have breath in my body, I should care for the living. I will be patient about the rest.' Father and daughter hugged each other in silent joy.

'Time we were on our way, Edward,' said Darke with a smile, pulling the policeman towards the door. 'If we hurry, we can catch the first train to town and indulge ourselves in the dining car.'

5

THE CURSE OF THE GRISWOLD PHANTOM

Dusk comes early to Griswold Mire. It is as though Nature itself cannot wait to hide this inhospitable place from the sight of man. With the darkness, the mist rises, seeping from the gurgling, slimy depths to wreathe the surface with white coils, which camouflage its treacherous surface. Luckless is the lonely wanderer who finds himself out by these marshes after sunset. One false step and he is sucked down, sucked down deep into the bottomless oozing darkness. But, as the locals know, there is another reason to fear the mire at night. It is the haunt of the Griswold Phantom.

With a sigh, Luther Darke dropped the letter he had been reading on to the breakfast table.

'It seems I am gaining a reputation, George,' he observed to his manservant while buttering his third piece of toast.

'That must be very gratifying, sir,' came the typically ambivalent reply.

'It would be if it were for my endeavours with a brush and palette. It now seems that I am beginning to attract lost causes.' He snatched up the letter again. 'Listen to this: "Dear Mr Darke, I write to you as my last resort." I must admit, George, that I have never been a last resort before. That part is quite appealing. "No doubt you will have read in the papers of the dreadful tragedy at Griswold. The police are quite baffled and, despite importing one of their top men from London, the mystery remains unsolved. I have read of your unofficial work for Scotland Yard, in particular your involvement in solving the murder of Lord Neville, and I wondered if you would be kind enough to investigate this matter yourself. I would be happy to pay you a retainer. Please let me know your feelings towards my request. I sense that our lives are in danger and I am at my wits' end. Yours sincerely, John Scarlett." What d'you make of that, George?'

'The gentleman appears somewhat desperate.'

'Desperate indeed. Clutching at straws, I would say.'

'Perhaps so, sir, but I would also note that the matter sounds rather intriguing.'

Darke laughed. 'To thine own self be true, and then thy man-servant cannot mock you with the truth. Of course it sounds intriguing. The request is seductive. And I am in need of some mental stimulation at the moment. For a few weeks now I've felt myself slipping into a mind-numbing malaise. This business could well revive me. What do you know of this Griswold matter? In fact, where is Griswold?'

'Griswold is a small coastal village in Suffolk.'

'Suffolk! The end of the earth. I certainly do not fancy travelling all the way to Suffolk to organise the arrest of the village grocer for poaching.'

'I gather that the matter in question is a little more serious than that, sir. According to what I have read in the papers, there has been a dreadful murder: a young woman was beheaded.'

'Not the village grocer, then. Very well, George, you have convinced me. I shall find out the details of the case – as we amateur sleuths call it. I'm sure my friend Inspector Thornton call fill me in on the background.'

She was conscious when it happened. Mercifully, it happened quickly. The dark figure loomed before her. Her eyes fell upon the scythe he was holding, the blade glistening in the bright moonlight. Terror froze the cry in her throat, and her mouth opened noiselessly. With a terrible surety, she knew exactly what was about to happen. The figure swung the scythe, its blade whistling through the cold night air. That whistling sound was the last she ever heard.

'Luther! What on earth are you doing here?' Automatically, Edward Thornton rose from his chair at his friend's approach.

'It certainly is a new experience for me. I have never been in a police canteen before,' Darke responded, glancing around him with interest.

'Take a seat and let me get you a mug of tea.'

'Tea!' Darke's face contorted with distaste. 'That corrosive brown liquid which emanates from India?'

Thornton smiled and nodded.

'Disgusting stuff. Rots the stomach, my friend. What about a nice bottle of Chablis?'

Thornton's smile turned into a chuckle. 'This is Scotland Yard, not the Savage Club, Luther. I doubt if Dolly or Sarah, our tea ladies, have ever seen a bottle of Chablis, let alone served it up. And it's hardly the ideal beverage to be consumed by our bobbies before they go on duty.'

Darke slapped his gloves down on the table in mock irritation and nodded gravely, but there was a mischievous twinkle in the eyes. 'Therefore, I shall remain dry during our converse.'

'Another unique experience. Two in one morning. That must be quite exciting.'

'My, the inspector is sharp today. I must be on my mettle.'

'How can I help you?'

'Good man. To the matter in hand. What can you tell me about this ugly business at Griswold?'

The policeman, about to take a drink, faltered and lowered the tin mug slowly, placing it on the table. 'What on earth has that to do with you?'

'Edward, you are developing feminine traits: answering one question with another. Just tell me what you know about the murder at Griswold.'

Thornton's eyes narrowed as he gazed suspiciously at his friend. What was the fellow up to now? 'Where do I start?'

'At the beginning. My knowledge of the affair is a blank canvas. Work the brushstrokes in for me.'

'Very well. Griswold is a little hamlet on the east coast, twenty miles from Ipswich. A young woman was murdered there about a week ago. She was found lying by the Griswold Mire; her head had been cut from her body.'

'A gruesome touch, indeed. Where was her head?'

'It has not been found. It is probably languishing in the depths of the mire. There is a legend in those parts concerning the curse of the Phantom Reaper of the Griswold Mire, a spectral creature who rises from the slime to behead the unwary who pass by his domain after nightfall.'

'A tall, ghostly, faceless fiend, attired in wet, tattered rags who emerges at sunset carrying a glistening scythe.'

'You know the curse?'

'Of course not. The term "phantom reaper" conjures up the image immediately. The stuff of childish nightmares and penny dreadfuls. Every area of the country has its ghostly dogs, headless horsemen, wicked will o' the wisps. They are cliché phantoms and as such are to be ignored by the rational mind – unless there is proof to the contrary.'

'Well, the dead body cannot be ignored.'

'Certainly. But you know as well as I that no boggy bogeyman – a thing of fable and fairytale – did such a deed. Has the woman been identified?'

'She was Emily Scarlett of…'

'The Grange, Griswold.'

Thornton's brow creased in surprise. 'Yes. So you do know all about the matter.'

Darke shook his head, 'No, no. Forgive me Edward. This morning I had a letter from a John Scarlett seeking my help.'

'The girl's father. Does he know you?'

'He knows of me – the "unofficial solver of riddles" as the *Evening Standard* referred to me after the Neville case. My fame seems to have spread as far as Suffolk. However, this appears to be a serious and desperate request. Apparently the police have made no progress in their investigation, despite the involvement of a top man from the Yard. Great Heavens, it's not you is it?'

'No it is not. Although I'm not saying I could have made any headway in the matter either. Barraclough's handling the case.'

'Oh, Barraclough. A decent enough fellow, I suppose, but with the imagination of a clockwork monkey. Well, never mind. Now, please resume your narrative. I promise not to interrupt again.'

'Very well.' Thornton drained his mug before continuing. 'You must realise that I can only give you the roughest of outlines. I only know what has been reported in the press and what has been the gossip around the Yard.'

Darke nodded.

'John Scarlett, a rich man, is a widow with three grown-up children, two of whom live with him at the Grange – or rather lived with him. There is a son Ralph, a fellow of eighteen or so, who I gather is blind. Then there was Emily, a pretty young woman by all accounts, who was not yet thirty. She had taken on the burden of being the lady of the house when her mother died some five years ago, carrying out many of the domestic duties. The third child, Charles, is in Terai running a tea plantation. The rest of the household is made up of the manservant and his wife, who acts as cook and housekeeper – I cannot recall their names. So, there you have the cast of the drama. The first event that led to the tragedy was the disappearance of the family pet, a golden-haired retriever. John Scarlett was in the habit of walking with the dog in the afternoon before tea. On one day, just over a week ago, the dog could not be found. A thorough search of the premises revealed nothing, so Scarlett, with his daughter and butler, set out to search for the creature. It was nearly dark when they returned from their fruitless quest. However, the dog was discovered the following morning by one of the villagers, the local vicar, I believe. He was walking by the Griswold Mire when he spied a strange yellow object floating by the reeds. It turned out to be the Scarletts' retriever. It had been beheaded.

'This atrocity greatly distressed the family, as might be expected, but it also started up rumours in the village that the dark reaper had returned. Beheading was his trademark. The curse dates from the Middle Ages, and even within living memory corpses have been found in the mire *sans* head. It has put the fear of God into the locals.'

Thornton paused for a moment. Darke, keeping his word, said nothing, but waited for the further instalment in this gruesome recital.

'It was not long before the second and more terrible blow fell upon the Scarlett family. They had been cheered by a letter from the eldest brother, who had sent news that he had sold his plantation and was returning home after being in India for nearly ten years. There seemed to be real cause for happiness and hope. And then Emily went missing. She failed to arrive at breakfast one morning and on investigation it was discovered that her bed had not been slept in the previous night. The local police were called in and a search was instigated. You may well deduce the outcome.'

'The girl was found on the edge of the mire with her head missing. Ill met by moonlight.'

'What is baffling everyone is that there appears to be no motive for these grotesque crimes. To my mind, the killing of the dog and the murder of Emily Scarlett have the taint of revenge upon them but neither John nor his son Ralph can think of anyone who has such a fierce grudge against the family.' Thornton paused and toyed with his empty mug for a moment before continuing. 'Now I think you know as much as I do, Luther. It's a strange affair, and I can tell you privately that I am rather glad it was Barraclough and not I who was sent to Suffolk. But tell me, seriously, are you really contemplating travelling up to Griswold and investigating this business?'

'After what you have told me, how could I resist? The affair is bizarre in the extreme: beheaded dogs, ghostly phantoms, a beleaguered family – and no clues. I presume there are no clues.'

Thornton afforded himself a gentle smile. 'Apparently Barraclough is as much in the dark as the local constabulary.'

'I thought as much. Clockwork monkeys do not solve mysteries.' Darke suddenly leaned over the table and touched the policeman's arm. 'There is another reason for my going, a reason that goes beyond my trifling passion for a puzzle. Here is a family in great trouble and I have been asked to help. Under the circumstances, there is no way I could refuse.'

'I just hope you don't get your fingers burned.'

'I shall wear asbestos gloves! Tell me one more thing before I depart. If the local belief is that the phantom reaper is responsible for these crimes, is there anyone who has claimed to have seen this murderous spectre?'

'Indeed. Several villagers. And John Scarlett himself.'

'I usually know when you are jesting with me, Luther. There is a kind of pleasing twinkle in your eye and you cannot prevent the corners of your mouth turning up a fraction. But I see neither of these telltale traits now. You really are being serious, aren't you?'

Luther Darke thought it wise to respond with a mere nod of the head.

Carla's voice rose an octave higher. 'Suffolk! Some godforsaken sleepy haven near nowhere. You want me to go to Suffolk with you to help you catch … what, a … spectral reaper?'

'A murderer.'

'Oh, don't be so dramatic, Luther. You are not a policeman, you are an artist. Leave this murderer to the local constabulary.'

Darke had expected this reaction from Carla and he was deliberately pacing himself with his attempt at persuasion. He had called at Carla's apartment in Bloomsbury just before lunch in the hope of enlisting her services as his companion on the Griswold investigation, but he knew that it would not be an easy task. Paradoxically, Carla was an instinctive free spirit, quixotic and spontaneous, but on her terms only. She hated to fall in with plans that had been arranged for her without any consultation.

'As you can see,' Carla's voice still bordered on the strident, 'I am fully engaged upon my novel and any disruption now could interfere with my flow.'

'My darling, pack your muse with you. You can still write on the train. I am sure the rhythm of the engine will enhance your flow.'

Carla's features softened. A flicker of warmth returned to her eyes.

'Such a journey, such an experience – think what it may contribute to the richness of your prose.'

Now her lips parted into a smile. Ah, the fish are biting, thought Darke.

'My darling, I am not writing a murder mystery but an elegant allegorical drama highlighting … well you know what it's highlighting.' The smile widened.

'It's a diatribe against the subservient role of women in society today.'

'It is!'

'So are you going to come with me or not, woman?'

'Of course I am, damn you!'

With that, Luther Darke swept her up into his arms and kissed her passionately on the lips.

John Scarlett received two telegrams that afternoon. Both gave details of arrivals. The first was from Luther Darke, indicating that he and Carla were journeying to Griswold and would be arriving at the local station around seven that evening. The second was from Charles, his eldest son, stating that his ship had docked in Southampton that very day and he was making arrangements to travel home as soon as possible. He hoped to arrive home on the morrow. Both messages brought a sense of comfort and hope to the old man. Little did he know that the comfort and the hope were destined to be short-lived.

Despite her acquiescence to accompany her lover on the trek to Suffolk, Carla had remained tight-lipped for most of the journey. It was only on the last leg, from Ipswich to Griswold, that she realised that Luther, who had also remained taciturn en route, was playing her at her own game. If there was to be a point to her being there, she needed to know the details of the matter.

Carla gazed out of the window and watched an orange sun begin to dip down below the silhouetted contours of the Suffolk countryside. She said softly, 'Tell me who died, how, any other relevant details and what you know that the police don't.'

'I'll tell you what I think I know but I probably know less than the police at present. However, I am confident that it will not take me long to catch up – and to overtake them.'

'There is a fine line between confidence and arrogance, darling. Take care not to overstep it.'

Reaching for his whisky flask, Luther Darke flashed Carla a broad grin and told her the story of the Griswold Phantom as he had learned it from Thornton. When he had finished, he leaned back in his carriage seat and awaited her reaction. She was silent and thoughtful for a moment before responding.

'I can see how this bizarre affair appeals to you. It has all the ghoulish charm of a Gothic tale by Mr Bram Stoker. Surely it is priests and exorcists the family need, instead of sleuths and puzzle solvers.'

'But it is not a Gothic tale, and in real life, ghostly phantoms do not behead the living. And certainly they do not restrict their ethereal homicide attacks to the inhabitants of one household, including its dog. There is too much practical crudity about these deaths. It is clear to me that there is human – rather than supernatural – evil at work here. I am convinced of it. I only hope I can lift away the veils that hide the truth before there is another death.'

Darke and Carla were met outside the small station at Griswold by Jacob Steerforth, the manservant at the Grange. He was a stout man of ruddy complexion. Beneath a pair of thick, shaggy eyebrows, which dominated the face, there peered out two sharp button eyes which shifted restlessly. He threw their cases unceremoniously into the back of a wagonette and helped Carla aboard. Within moments they were rattling away into the darkness towards the Grange.

It was difficult to hold a conversation above the clatter of hooves and the shaking of the wagon, and Steerforth seemed happier to remain silent, but Luther Darke was determined to glean some pieces of information from the man.

'Tell me, Steerforth,' he cried, leaning close to the man's ear, 'have you ever seen this Grim Reaper I've heard so much about?'

At first the man did not reply and then after easing the pace of the horses he turned a broad face to his interrogator, the black eyes flickering with emotion. 'That I have. And I never want to see the same sight again as long as I live.'

'Will you tell me about it?'

'I'd rather not…'

'But it may help in my investigation – you know I'm coming to the Grange to try and help solve the mystery of Miss Scarlett's death.'

Steerforth nodded. 'You'll not do that, sir. Her death weren't natural. It was the Reaper.'

'Then tell me about him, man.'

There was a brusqueness in Darke's tone that surprised and rather unnerved Steerforth. It was a calculated brusqueness, but the servant was not to know that and it achieved its purpose. Steerforth gave a cough of irritation and nodded. 'Very well. It was on my day off. Greta, my wife, was out of sorts, so I took myself off to Ipswich to look up some old friends. I came back late-ish and decided to walk from the station and take the shortcut by the mire. As I was passing that godforsaken place … well, that's when I saw him … it.'

'The Griswold Phantom?'

'Yes.'

'Where exactly was he?'

'Some way from the firm ground. Out in the mire, as though he was standing on it.'

'Describe him.'

'He was tall, wearing one of those hooded things that monks wear, and he was carrying a scythe. It seemed to glow in the darkness. In fact there seemed to be a shimmering light outlining his whole figure. I don't know how, but I knew that he had seen me. His head turned in my direction and then … and then…' Steerforth gulped for breath, as though he was too frightened to continue.

'What happened?' prompted Darke.

'Then, as God is my witness, he started to walk towards me, very slowly, across the surface of the mire. No living man can do that. He was coming to claim me, I'm sure. I ran. I ran like the wind. I ran until my heart nearly thrust its way through my chest. I carried on until I was indoors at the Grange and then I double-bolted the door behind me.'

'Are you convinced that the Phantom claimed the life of Emily Scarlett?'

'I am. We are dealing with the Devil's agent in Griswold, and God have mercy on all our souls.'

The Grange was a large, rambling house about a mile from the village. It was clear to Darke that the original dwelling, probably Tudor in origin, had been added to at least twice in different periods, resulting in an ugly, disjointed frontage which the straggly, weather-beaten ivy that crept across its brickwork failed to disguise. It was perched some four hundred yards from the cliff edge, which fell away sharply to the pebbled beach below.

Steerforth unloaded the bags and led Darke and Carla into the hallway, where they were met by a pale-faced woman who was introduced as the housekeeper, Greta, Steerforth's wife.

'Show the guests to their room and I will inform Mr John of their arrival.'

Greta nodded, and without a word swept up the staircase. The weary travellers followed.

Their room was tidy and clean, but rather bleak. Greta turned back the bed.

'Thank you,' said Carla in an attempt to break the chilly silence.

Greta made some soft inarticulate response and left the room.

'One gets the impression that the staff are not terribly enamoured of our presence,' said Darke slumping down on the bed.

'I see I do not get my own room. I end up playing your wife again.'

'But you are so good in the part, my sweet.'

Carla moved to the window and looked out. The room was at the front of the house and overlooked the lawn and the small copse that ran to the wall of the grounds. It was a moonlit night, and the silver beams touched the foliage with what appeared to be a feathery silver ash. It was a strange and alien landscape of grey and white, as though it had been sketched by Gustave Doré. Suddenly Carla stiffened and, involuntarily, she gave a little gasp as her hand flew to her mouth in shock and surprise.

'What is it?' cried Darke rushing to her side. He gazed out of the window and saw the reason for his lover's consternation. There on the lawn below was a figure darting away from the house towards the shrubbery. It was impossible to see his face, but the long cloak that billowed out behind him seemed to glow in the darkness. The figure was carrying a large scythe that also shimmered with an unnatural glow.

'What on earth was that?' whispered Carla, as the ghostlike creature disappeared into the bushes and out of sight.

'Obviously it was the Griswold Phantom.' Before Darke had a chance to elaborate on his response, there came an urgent knocking at the door and Jacob Steerforth's voice cried out, 'Mr Darke, Mr Darke, sir, please come quickly. The master's disappeared.'

Darke wrenched the door open. 'What exactly do you mean "disappeared"?'

'He's … he's not in his study or the sitting room. I can't think that he would have left the house now it's gone dark.'

'When did you last see him?'

'Just before I set off to the station to collect you, sir.'

'Have you spoken to Ralph Scarlett? Perhaps a message was left with him.'

'No, no, I haven't. No doubt he'll be in his room having a rest.'

'Then, nil desperandum, Steerforth, old chap, let's check up on the young master.'

'I'm coming with you,' said Carla, pulling her shawl more tightly around her shoulders. The image of the creature on the lawn was still floating vividly in her consciousness and she had no desire to be left alone in this draughty, ill-lit old house.

Darke took her hand and gave it a squeeze. 'Lay on, Macduff,' he said to Steerforth, who led them back along the corridor and down the staircase into the hallway. At this moment the main door opened and a young man entered. He was tall and exceedingly thin, with the complexion of one who spends much of his time indoors. His eyes were a whitish, watery blue and it was clear that they gave him no sight.

'Master Ralph,' exclaimed the butler in a heated fashion.

'What is it, Steerforth?'

'Your father is missing.'

'Nonsense. He will be in the house somewhere. Have you tried the library?'

Steerforth hesitated. 'No, sir.'

'There then, how can he be missing? He'll be holed up in there with a book.'

At this point Luther Darke stepped forward and introduced himself and Carla. The young man nodded, giving Darke a limp handshake. 'My father told me that he had written to you. To be honest, I fail to see the point. You are not a detective, are you?'

'I am not a professional detective, but I came to help.'

The young man's features softened. 'It was not my intention to be rude, Mr Darke, but the death of my sister has put us under an immense amount of strain, and such niceties as courtesy and manners are easily forgotten under such circumstances.'

'I understand perfectly. I only came because I think I may be able to assist in clearing up this mystery.'

'If only you could.'

'Let's find your father first. Shall we try the library?'

On entering the library, they found that a solitary candelabrum was the only gloomy source of illumination. The candles flickered unnaturally, bathing the book-lined room in a gentle wash of yellow light. Jacob Steerforth stepped forward and clicked the electric switch. Immediately the room sprang to attention as the vivid Swan & Edgar lamps flooded the chamber in harsh brightness. Now they could see properly.

Now they could see the dead body lying by the window.

'My God,' cried Steerforth. 'Mr Scarlett.' He knelt by the corpse and gave a heart-rending moan of anguish. 'Oh, no,' he sobbed.

'What is it?' cried Ralph, attempting to push his way past the visitors, but Darke held him back. 'No, sir. No further. Your father has been attacked. It is best if you stay here until I can ascertain what has actually happened, and then we must call for the police.'

'Attacked? We must get a doctor … he is … he is still alive?'

Steerforth looked at Darke and shook his head.

'I am afraid not,' said Darke softly. 'Carla, take Ralph off and find him a brandy or something. I need some time alone here with Steerforth.'

Without a word, Carla took the young man's arm and guided him from the room. His face was whiter than ever, the shock robbing him of all speech.

Darke knelt by the body. It was laid on its front, and the head was missing. A pool of sticky blood oozed out of the severed neck.

'The Phantom,' hissed Steerforth.

Darke made no comment, but pulled back the curtains to reveal that one of the windows was slightly open. 'This was where the devil escaped,' he muttered, almost to himself.

'It was the Phantom all right.'

'Was it? I thought that the legend told of this creature rising from the mire to attack those who dare pass by his lair after sunset. Is there anything in the legend which says that the Phantom makes personal calls?'

'What do you mean?'

'If this atrocity was really committed by the Phantom Reaper, then no man or woman is safe in their own home. It will not do, Steerforth. There is a human agency afoot here, and they have just made their first big mistake.'

'I was in the process of packing my bags. I was due to catch the midnight train back to London. I thought my work here was done.' Inspector Barraclough lit a cigarette and gazed down at the remains of John Scarlett. 'Poor blighter,' he added, as an afterthought.

Darke pursed his lips non-committally. He didn't care for Barraclough. He had none of the sharpness and flexibility of mind that Thornton possessed. On top of that, the man had an arrogant swagger, which he used to cover his ignorance and lack of perception.

'What I can't understand is what you're doing here, Mr Darke. Are you a friend of the family?'

'Not exactly. But I was invited. Tell me, have you any theories, any clues as to who is behind these crimes?'

Barraclough hesitated for a moment, staring down at the mutilated corpse, and then, deciding to be honest about the matter, shook his head. 'No. But I can tell you that I haven't fallen in with the local view that there's a homicidal phantom abroad.' He gave a little snort of derision. 'Though there might as well be, for I've learned nothing in Griswold. There seems to be no clear motive.'

'There is always a motive for murder, and sometimes it is so obvious that it is easily overlooked.'

'So you think I've overlooked it?' There was irritation in the inspector's voice.

'I think you haven't recognised it. But neither have I – yet.'

'Well, that's a great help.'

'There is little to be done tonight. If you could arrange for the body to be removed, and then in the morning, what say if you and I take a walk by the Griswold Mire and see if we can spot anything?'

'If you like.'

'Call round at ten and we'll take the air together.'

After the inspector left and the corpse of John Scarlett had been removed to the police station, Darke and Carla ate a desultory meal in the sombre dining room served by a moist-eyed Greta. Ralph had retired to his room with a sedative, his grief only partly realised. He appeared not to fully grasp the fact that he had now lost a father as well as a sister within the space of a few days.

For most of the time Darke was silent and withdrawn. Between courses, he examined the various portraits of the Scarlett family which adorned the panelled walls. Carla was used to these sudden bouts of introspection and easily lost herself in her own thoughts.

Darke consumed a bottle of claret during the meal, and when it came time for brandy and coffee, he invited Jacob Steerforth to join them.

'Tell me, Steerforth,' he said, after pouring the servant a large brandy which matched his own, 'Mr Scarlett was a rich man. How did he acquire his wealth?'

'He had been a very successful merchant banker, but he retired after suffering a mild stroke some ten years ago. He recovered fully, but he found life in the country more to his liking.'

'How long have you worked for him?'

'Since he came here. He set me and my wife on when he moved into the Grange. I've lived in this area the best part of my life.'

'You have no family of your own?'

'We had a son but we lost him to the fever when he was only fourteen. That was around twenty year ago.'

'I am so sorry.'

'Life deals many cruel cards. We've learned to live with it, Greta and I.'

'Indeed.' Darke was quiet for a moment, his saturnine features held immobile in thought. Then, with a quick smile, he addressed Steerforth again. 'But John – was he a good master?

'He was a good master and a good man.'

'Even good men have enemies.'

Steerforth shook his head. 'He had none to my knowledge.'

'There was no mention of any business rivals from the old days?'

'No.'

'Who inherits his fortune?'

'The bulk goes to his family. No doubt Charles will receive the lion's share.'

'Ah, the prodigal who returns home tomorrow.'

'Yes, and what a dreadful homecoming that will be. His dear father and sister gone. The poor devil. He was the apple of his father's eye, was Charles. The young man will be most dreadfully upset.'

'When did he go out to Terai?'

'Oh, it'll be nearly ten years, I should think.'

'And he's not been back since?'

'No.'

'So you have never met him.'

'That is true.'

'I notice that there is no portrait of Charles, and yet the rest of the family are here.' Darke swung his arm in a theatrical manner to encompass the portraits that stared down at them. 'I understand these were done about a year after Charles went abroad.'

Steerforth nodded. 'That's right, sir.'

'Pity. There is a suitable space for such a portrait – should it be painted – over by the fireplace.'

'Indeed.'

Darke shifted his gaze to another painting. That of the youngest son. 'Tell me about young Ralph. Was he blind from birth?'

'So I gather. He's a weak sop of a youth, I'm afraid. He was a great disappointment to his father. Don't get me wrong, there was no bad blood between 'em, but the lad has always seemed trapped in his world of darkness and made no real attempt to cope with his disability. He spends his days walking on the cliffs in all weathers or just sitting, staring, as it were, into space. He's never made a friend in his life.'

'What a sad creature,' said Carla softly. She had been sitting in the shadows and Steerforth had all but forgotten her presence, so wrapped up was he in his conversation with Darke.

'A sadder one now his father has gone, Mrs Darke.'

Carla shuddered at this appellation, but refrained from denying it. 'Time for bed, darling, I think,' she said pointedly.

Darke, pouring himself another large brandy, nodded in agreement. 'It will be a pleasure to put this sorrowful day behind us.'

On retiring to their room, Darke sat on the bed, savouring the brandy. 'This is a complex affair, my sweet. I can well understand why the redoubtable Inspector Barraclough feels like a blind man in a coal cellar.'

Carla yawned and slipped under the covers. 'It might have been wiser to have stayed in London.'

'No, no, my dear. You misunderstood me when I said that it was complex. I did not mean to imply that it was baffling.'

'Oh, so you've solved the mystery, have you?'

'I have a theory at least, but I shall need more data to test it out, and I shall have to give more thought to the three Ms.'

'The three Ms?'

'Motive, Method and Mistake. All murderers have a motive and a method, and they all make a mistake.'

'But not all murderers are caught.'

Darke drained the brandy glass. 'That is because their mistake has not been recognised. In this case, however, our murderer or murderers will be caught.'

'If you say so,' said Carla dreamily, as she snuggled down.

Darke kissed her lightly on the cheek. 'Sweet phantomless dreams to you, my love.'

Carla did not respond. She had already drifted off to sleep.

Barraclough arrived at the Grange early the next morning, and shortly afterwards he and Luther Darke took an expedition to the mire. It was indeed a grim place. The air was filled with a pungent, sulphurous aroma and the green undulating surface of the mire was broken at irregular intervals by grey stagnant pools, which intermittently bubbled and belched. Darke was sensitive to locations and at first glance, the place made him shudder.

Dramatic and unscientific though the thought was, he sensed that there was something intrinsically evil about the place. And, he reasoned, he was seeing it in bright morning sunshine; he could only imagine the unsettling aura the place must have at dusk.

'Nasty place,' said Barraclough, as though he had been reading his companion's thoughts.

'Hell is murky,' said Darke, picking up a stone and hurling it out into the seething morass. It plopped into one of the stagnant pools and slipped from sight. 'Tell me, Inspector Barraclough, you have interviewed some of the villagers about the Phantom Reaper?'

'In the pursuit of my duty, yes, but as you know I hold no...'

'Did any of them say they saw the fiend walk upon the mire as Christ walked upon the waters of Galilee?'

'Walk upon ...? Not that I recall. The main tale was of shimmering lights after dark. One or two vowed they had seen what looked like a glowing figure. But no one claimed to have actually seen the Reaper.'

'I thought so.'

Carla was reading by the fire in the library when Ralph Scarlett entered. He looked paler and more haggard than he had the previous day. He moved unsteadily, more through nervousness, thought Carla, than because of his lack of sight. He took a chair opposite her, near the fire.

'I have come to apologise,' he said, so quietly that Carla was not sure she had heard clearly what he had said.

'Apologise?' She was puzzled.

'To begin with, for my behaviour on your arrival. I was beastly to you and your husband, especially when you had travelled here to help us and then ... and then for acting like a complete idiot when my father was found. I ... I should have taken charge. I should have acted with courage. Instead I did what I always do: I gave in to my emotions. No wonder my father despised me. I was the runt of the litter, the weak, useless one. If only I could have been like Charles. Decisive, self-assured, brave. But of course, he could see.'

Throughout this speech, the youth had been on the verge of tears and now they came, running down his hollow cheeks. Instinctively, Carla reached out to comfort him. As her hand brushed his, he flinched, drawing back.

'I'm disgracing myself further,' he murmured in self-derision, 'weeping like a child.'

'You have lost a sister and a father in the most dreadful circumstances,' said Carla, softly. 'Anyone with any sensitivity would be upset. It is a perfectly natural reaction. What is not natural is to blame yourself for being weak. If such a thing had happened to me, I would probably be running around the garden cursing God for his unfairness. I should have to be restrained.'

'But you are a woman.'

'So?' Carla's voice was now sharp as steel. 'Women do not hold the exclusive rights to genuine and personal unfettered emotion, you know. Men are allowed to cry, feel pain, anguish and despair just as much as women are. It is the breed of men who sublimate these perfectly natural feelings, denying their humanity, who are restricting the development of society. Paradoxically, they are the weak ones for denying their own emotions. There is nothing wrong in expressing genuine feelings. True emotion, true passion, is the key to personal honesty.' She stopped abruptly, suddenly aware that she had climbed upon her soapbox, and in realisation of this she giggled. 'I'm sorry. I must sound like a political tract.'

Ralph permitted himself a smile. 'I suppose so, but I've never heard anyone speak like that before. It sounds so sensible, but all that I've ever been told all my life is to face things like a man.'

'And of course you should – but it is the definition of man that is faulty. By man, they meant some kind of impenetrable fortress of masculinity where softer feelings, sensitivity and true emotion were outlawed.'

Ralph nodded. 'I believe you are right.'

Luther Darke, who had entered the room some moments earlier and had been standing in the shadows by the door observing, stepped forward now and laid a hand upon the youth's shoulders. 'It is my experience, sir,' he said seriously, 'that this lady is invariably correct.'

Ralph nodded. 'Mr Darke, I wondered how long it would be before you announced yourself.'

Darke grinned and cast an arched glance at Carla. 'And I thought I had been so discreet.'

'A blind man has a developed sense of hearing.'

'Of course. I was wondering, Mr Scarlett, if you were feeling well enough to answer a few of my questions.'

'For your investigation.' The voice had grown sullen again and was edged with sarcasm.

'To help clarify a few details, at least.'

'Very well. It would be as my father wished, no doubt; although I have no idea what I can tell you that will be of any help.'

'Let's see, shall we?'

Ralph Scarlett nodded.

'Can you think of anyone who has a particular grudge against this family – or your father in particular?'

'No. My father was successful and wealthy, but he was also compassionate and well-liked. There's no evil business rival waiting in the wings, if that's what you're implying.'

'Not really. Do you have any theories of your own?'

'I thought you were the detective. No, I don't. The only thing that seems certain is that I'm next on the list, or Charles, when he arrives.'

'When was the last time you saw your brother?'

'I have never seen my brother, Mr Darke. I have been blind from birth. I remember very little of him now. I was at boarding school at the time he left for Terai. It will be like meeting a stranger. On the other hand, he and Emily were very close. It's very difficult generating intimacies when you can't see, you know.'

At this moment, the door burst open and Steerforth rushed in, clutching a sheet of cream paper. On seeing the little tableau by the window and realising that he was interrupting a private conversation, he faltered in his steps. 'Oh, I'm sorry Master Ralph, I didn't know you were with the guests.'

'Don't worry, Steerforth. This isn't private: it's detective work. Anyway, what is it, man? You rattled in here as though the house was on fire.'

'It's a telegram, sir. From your brother, Charles. He arrives by the mid-day train.'

Inspector Barraclough and Luther Darke met Charles Scarlett at Griswold Halt at noon. Scarlett was a lean, tanned young man whose sandy hair was already thinning. He was surprised and initially bemused by his welcoming committee. After brief introductions, Barraclough led him to the small stationmaster's office which had been vacated specially for the interview. 'What is this all about, Inspector? You are acting in a very mysterious way.'

In a halting and, as Darke thought, a somewhat inadequate fashion, Barraclough told Charles Scarlett the events of the tragedy that had blighted his family. Darke saw disbelief and then horror grow in the young man's eyes as he listened to Barraclough's narrative. When the inspector had finished, Charles Scarlett clutched his sleeve. 'This is true, isn't it? It is not some monstrous kind of joke?'

'It is the monstrous truth, Mr Scarlett,' said Darke, grabbing Barraclough's arm. 'I think we should leave our friend alone for a moment to compose himself.'

'No, no,' cried Charles Scarlett angrily. 'I do not need time "to compose myself". I just want to go home.'

'Well, I don't mind admitting to you, Mr Darke, that this is the strangest and most … I don't know … baffling, I suppose is the word… baffling case I've handled. Although I've not really handled it, if you get my meaning.'

It was an hour later and Darke and Barraclough were ensconced in the parlour of The Raven's Wing, a hostelry in Griswold. They had thought it politic to allow Charles Scarlett to return home alone without a policeman and a stranger present. Luther Darke was happy with this arrangement, for he knew that Carla would be there to note what happened when the prodigal stepped through the front door. It also gave him time to down a few single malt whiskies with his new friend Inspector Barraclough, or 'Cedric, please' as it became after two pints of the local ale. Darke liked village alehouses: the fug, the warmth, the kindness of the gas lighting that threw gentle rounded shadows and the general bonhomie of the patrons.

On his fourth pint, Barraclough's coherence was failing fast. 'I'm throwing in the trowel … er, towel, I can tell you, Mishter Darke. There is simply nothing to go on. I got to hand this case back to the chaps at Ipswich. I'm wasting my time up here. I should be back in London sorting out a stabbing in Houndsditch.'

Darke nodded sagely. As usual, the six glasses of spirits had warmed his inside, but had not dulled his brain. Indeed, they had sharpened it.

'So if you'll excuse me,' continued the bleary-eyed policeman, getting to his feet, somewhat unsteadily, 'I'll go to my hotel and pack my bags.' He half-turned to leave and then faced Darke again and stuck out his hand. A sly inebriated grin fixing itself on his face, he said in a voice that was louder than necessary, 'The best of luck with The Phantom. Look out he doesn't get you.'

Suddenly Darke's eyes sparkled. 'What a good idea,' he cried grabbing Barraclough's outstretched hand. The grin vanished and his eyes blinked in drunken confusion. 'Have a safe journey, Inspector.'

On wavering legs, Barraclough made his way to the door of the inn. Darke followed him as far as the bar, where he leaned forward and attracted the landlord's attention.

'What's it to be, sir? The same again?'

Darke nodded and sipped some coins on the counter. Cradling his new drink, he turned and rested with his back to the bar. 'Tell me, Mr Tandy, who is that old gentleman sitting by the inglenook?'

'How d'you know my name?' came the landlord's brusque reply.

'Because you advertise the fact in a sign above the door. A simple observation.'

'Oh, aye,' said the landlord slowly, as though he thought such stuff was the work of the devil.

'The old gentleman…' prompted Darke, reminding Tandy of his original query.

'Ah, that be Able Squires. Almost part of the fixture and fittings in here, is old Abe.'

'What is his tipple? Beer?'

'Porter, sir, the blacker the better.'

'Very well, draw a tankard of porter for me. I intend to treat old Abe.'

Able Squires awoke from his reverie to find a tall, saturnine stranger standing by him with a pint of porter in one hand.

'Would you do the honour of supping with me, Mr Squires?' said the stranger with a pleasant, mellifluous voice.

The old man looked at his own tankard, which was almost empty, and then back at the one that was being proffered by the stranger and nodded. He took the drink from Darke with a smile. 'That be right kind of ye, but I be puzzled why you should be spending your money on me, sir. We be strangers to one another.'

Darke matched Abe's smile and drew up a chair. 'Perhaps you can give me some information in return.'

Able took a long deep drink of the porter, draining almost a quarter of the tankard in one go. He was left with a dark smear on his upper lip that he wiped with the sleeve of his jacket. 'What information might that be? I reckon I know nothing that would be useful to a gentleman like yourself.'

'I think you underestimate yourself, Mr Squires. You have lived in these parts for many years?'

Able Squires chuckled. 'I was born not a stone's throw from here and lived in Griswold all me days, and they've mounted up into a lot o' years – eighty-three of 'em, come next May Day.'

'You would be a walking history of this village then?'

'That I am.' The old man screwed his wrinkled face into what was virtually a toothless grin. 'There's nothing much 'appens around here that I don't know the what of.' The thought pleased him so much that he drained his tankard dry.

'It is as I thought,' said Darke. 'Let me get you another drink and then perhaps you'd be kind enough to answer a few questions.'

'Of course I can. It's the least I can do for your unbounded generosity, sir.' So saying, he held out his tankard like a wizened Oliver Twist.

While Luther Darke was entertaining Able Squires, Carla was having an uncomfortable interview with Charles Scarlett. She had spent the morning in the library working on her novel, although she had found it difficult to shut out thoughts of the tragedy that hovered over the house like a dark thundercloud, which at any moment might loose a deadly flash of lightning. Shortly before noon, her literary endeavours had been interrupted by the presence of a tall, suntanned, handsome-looking man in a creased linen suit. He introduced himself as Charles Scarlett.

'I gather you are the wife of the man my father sent for to help solve this…' For a moment he seemed lost for words and then added, 'to discover the reason behind these tragic deaths.'

Once again, despite the gravity of the situation, Carla could not help feel the stabbing pinprick of irritation at being called Luther's wife. She loved him dearly but would never marry him; nor, she thought, did he wish her to marry him. They were both too idiosyncratic for such an arrangement, and besides, marriage implied ownership, a concept that was abhorrent to her. But what offended her sensibilities was the assumption that because she was a woman and accompanied by a man, they must be man and wife. With an intake of breath, she sublimated all these feelings to answer the main point of Charles Scarlett's question.

'Yes. Luther came here in response to your father's desperate plea. In London, he has become something of a celebrity for solving apparently unsolvable puzzles.' Carla could have almost bitten off her tongue as she spoke. She could hear how pompous and superficial her words were. Here was a man who had lost his father and sister in a set of grisly murders, and she was talking about 'unsolvable puzzles' as though she was referring to a parlour card trick.

Scarlett's face registered his distaste at her facile explanation. 'Well,' he said sternly, 'it appears that Mr Darke has been spectacularly unsuccessful in his efforts. Since his arrival my father has also lost his life. I do not wish to be rude, nor indeed inhospitable, but as the new head of the household I would appreciate it if you and your husband could arrange to return to London forthwith. You will appreciate that this is a household in mourning, and the intrusion of strangers … need I say more?'

Carla nodded. 'I understand. As soon as Mr Darke returns, we will make arrangements to leave.'

Charles Scarlett gave her a tight grin and turned on his heel.

Some minutes later, as Carla was putting some of her clothes into her suitcase, there came a gentle knock at the door. On answering it, she discovered Ralph Scarlett standing hesitantly on the threshold.

'I'm sorry to disturb you, but I've just heard that Charles has asked you to leave. I'm very sorry.'

'It is probably for the best,' said Carla, taking the young man's hand.

'You … you have been so kind to me; I don't want you to go. My brother is being unreasonable.'

'He is probably in shock. You will have to give him time for his mind to accept all the dreadful events that have happened.'

'I suppose so. I so looked forward to his return, but … but his behaviour has been so brusque. It is like he is a harsh stranger to me.'

'He has been away from this house for ten years. In a sense, both you and he are strangers now. You've lived with the terrible truth of your sister and your father's deaths for longer than he has. You are now the strong one, Ralph. You are the one who has to build the bridge between you again.'

'I am the strong one...?'

Carla smiled and gave him a kiss on the cheek. 'The strong one,' she affirmed. 'Now, tell your brother that I will work in my room until nightfall, when I hope Luther will return. I'll take my evening meal with Greta in the kitchen and then Luther and I will depart first thing in the morning.'

'Very well.' His gaunt features softened into a thin smile and he touched the cheek where Carla had kissed him. 'Thank you,' he said, and left her.

Inspector Cedric Barraclough was almost sober again. The walk back to the hotel and the effort of packing had dissipated the alcoholic haze somewhat. He was trying desperately to close the lid on his suitcase when he heard a discreet knock at the door.

'What is it?' he cried irritably, a fine sheen of sweat misting his brow.

'The solution to your investigation,' came the muffled response.

Leaving the lid of his case to spring free, depositing certain items back onto the bed, he pulled open the door. There on the threshold, holding his cloak across the lower part of his face in dramatic fashion, was Luther Darke.

'What game are you playing now?' he said with some petulance. Darke dropped the cloak. 'The game of catch-the-murderer. All the pieces have slotted into place now, Inspector, and I invite you to my arresting party. Are you game?'

An hour later, as the light began to die, a lone constable made his way up the driveway of the Grange. Constable Jem Burrows, a local lad who, although made of stern stuff, was still apprehensive about being so close to the mire and this cursed family home as dusk fell. He had grown up with the stories of the Phantom Reaper, and so vivid was the impression that these had made upon his consciousness, that all rationality was squashed. He really believed in such a creature. It was with some relief that he reached the lighted porch of the Grange. He tugged the ancient bell-pull and heard a responding clanking sound from somewhere inside the house. Moments later, Jacob Steerforth's broad face appeared around the corner of the door. His face registered surprise on seeing the young constable.

'The police, is it? What trouble do you bring now, lad?'

'I have a message.' He broke off to recall the exact words he'd been told to recite and then began again. 'I have an urgent message for Mister Charles Scarlett. He has to come with me immediately. We have news of the Reaper.'

Steerforth's eyes widened in surprise. 'What news?'

'I cannot say. Mr Scarlett must come with me … failure to do so would put … er, place him in breach of the law.'

The old servant's face clouded with apprehension, but he gave the policeman a reluctant nod. 'Wait here. I'll go and fetch the master.'

Left alone, Constable Burrows smiled. He'd managed the most difficult part of his duties without too much trouble. At least he hoped that it was the most difficult part. Again he shivered as he thought about the marshes.

'How did you find out about this place?' Barraclough swung his bull's eye lantern around the enclosed space and despite its feeble finger of light, it revealed a treasure trove.

'By cunning, kindness and two pints of porter,' replied Darke, cheerfully.

Charles Scarlett grunted with displeasure as Steerforth helped him on with his overcoat. 'What is all this damned nonsense about?' he snarled at Constable Burrows, who had now been allowed into the hall.

Once more, in ill-concealed parrot fashion, the young police-man explained: 'I am not at liberty to divulge the … the destination of our mission at this juncture; only to say that it is imperative that you accompany me.'

'Where on earth to?'

'I am not at liberty to divulge…'

'If that clown Barraclough is having me on some kind of wild goose chase, I'll see that his superiors learn about it, post haste. Now I am master of the Grange, I am not without influence.'

'Shall I come with you, sir?' asked Steerforth, who was clearly also disturbed by this unexpected turn of events.

Before Charles Scarlett could respond, Constable Burrows piped up again. 'That is not possible, sir. The instructions are that Mr Scarlett should accompany me alone.'

'Instructions! I'll give that jumped up incompetent "instruc-tions" when I see him.'

'Which will not be too long now, Mr Scarlett. So if you are ready, we'll make haste, if you please.'

It was now dark. The sky was clear of clouds, and the deep blue star-pricked sky seemed to press down on the flat Suffolk coun-tryside. The moon was low in the sky, but its pale beams threw a ghostly light onto that desolate spot. Already, a miasmic white mist was rising from the treacherous waste of the Griswold Mire. A persistent icy breeze, which swept in from the sea, played gently with the coiling tendrils of the mist. It was to this dread place that Constable Jem Burrows was leading Charles Scarlett. Although he had been absent from this terrain for many years, Scarlett knew the track they were following. What it all meant, he did not know, but a knot of fear was slowly tightening within his breast. He knew it would be futile to ask the young bobby why they were taking this path. He would only receive further versions of his learned responses, and he also felt sure that the constable was, to a large extent, as much in the dark about this matter as he was.

Both men carried storm lanterns that shone brightly in the dusk like giant bobbing fireflies, throwing an aura of amber light around them as they trudged single file along the path. At last the mire came into view, its wetness shining in the moonlight.

'What happens now, Constable?' Scarlett rasped, his body wracked with a mixture of fury and fear. There was no response to his question. 'I said, what happens…' On a sudden instinctive impulse, Scarlett swung around. There was no one there. The young constable had disappeared.

Puzzlement soon subsided into terror. Here he was, alone, totally alone, in the dark, out by the Griswold Mire. He had been lured here for heaven knows what purpose. Then he heard a sound ahead of him. It was like a muffled cry, but he could not be sure exactly what it was. In fact, he could not be sure he had heard anything, other than the wind. He scrambled further along the path until he found himself on the very edge of the mire, his feet sinking into squelching mud. Scarlett gave a cry of disgust and he stumbled forward, landing on his hands and knees. Something within him made him look up at that moment. And then he saw it. He saw it with a clarity that nearly froze his heart. He saw the Griswold Phantom.

Standing some twelve feet away from Charles Scarlett was a tall, dark, cowled figure, shimmering with the foul ooze of the mire. In its hand it held a long scythe, the blade of which glistened brightly in the creamy moonlight.

Scarlett gave out a shriek of terror that echoed over the wide expanse of the marsh like the lone cry of a wounded animal. Frantically he attempted to scramble to his feet, but fell to the ground again when the apparition began to move forward, its arm thrust out in a threatening gesture towards him.

'Stay … murderer. Stay,' came the weird, reedy voice which emanated from the darkened cowl.

'No,' Scarlett cried, lurching forward. It was as though his worst nightmares were coming true.

The Phantom loomed closer and repeated the word, 'Murderer.'

Scarlett attempted a response, but the only sound to escape from his mouth was a kind of strangulated moan.

The Griswold Phantom spoke again. 'You are a murderer, are you not, Thomas Steerforth?'

At the mention of his name, his real name, the man rose to his unsteady feet and in a wild, desperate attempt to escape, plunged forward into the mire.

'After him,' cried the Phantom, its voice more direct and less ethereal now. Two police constables, one of whom was Jem Burrows, emerged out of the darkness and grappled with the man, dragging him back from the avaricious clutches of Griswold Mire. Behind them appeared the bluff figure of Inspector Barraclough.

The constables wrested their struggling captive onto firmer ground.

'Get the cuffs on him, lads,' he said with some satisfaction, a grim smile touching his features.

Meanwhile, the Phantom Reaper was disrobing. Having dropped his scythe to the ground, he pulled off the stinking, slimy cowled robe with a cry of disgust. 'I must smell like a crate of rotten kippers,' observed Luther Darke with disdain, flinging the foul garment into the mire.

'You'll live,' said Barraclough. 'A good bath and a hot toddy will soon see you right as rain.'

'You have a very simplistic outlook, Inspector, but on this occasion, I suspect you are not far from the truth. Now shall we take this malfeasant back to the Grange and round up the rest of the gang?'

On arriving back at the Grange, Jacob and Greta Steerforth greeted the party with silent, white-faced shock. Without explanation, Darke led them all into the sitting room and Barraclough summoned Carla and Ralph to join them.

Jacob slumped down in a chair, his hands twitching nervously.

'Take it easy, old man,' said Darke. 'You should be pleased that we return your son to you, safe from the slimy jaws of the Griswold Mire.'

The servant shook his head in disbelief. 'What does this mean?'

'It means that the game is up,' said Barraclough. At this statement, Greta burst into tears and made to leave the room, but with a nod from Darke, Carla gently barred her way.

Ralph Scarlett stepped forward. 'Mr Darke, I am at a loss as to what is going on. Carla tells me that the police are here and that brother Charles is in handcuffs. I must ask you to explain this bizarre situation at once.' His voice was firm and measured and he spoke with a new authority.

'Indeed. Please sit down, everyone, while I endeavour to untangle this grisly knot,' said Darke, pouring himself a liberal glass of whisky from the decanter.

'For a start, Mr Scarlett, the man in handcuffs is not your brother Charles. He is in fact Thomas Steerforth, the son of your family servant Jacob. This man has no more been in India than I. Certainly his face is brown – some facial dye no doubt, but he was careless not to treat the back of his hands in the same fashion. They are fair. The hands of anyone living in the hot climate of India for ten years would be nut brown. I am afraid to say that your brother is most likely dead – died out in Terai, I should say. Isn't that correct, Jacob?'

The retainer stared defiantly back at Darke but said nothing.

'Now, the story I am about to tell only deals roughly with the facts as I perceive them. No doubt in due course our fine trio – one must not forget Greta's involvement in the grand plan – will be obliged to add the detail, the minutiae. But as an artist I can give you a broad outline, essential features supported by some nuggets of information and a stimulated imagination.

'It must be that some time ago a telegram arrived for John Scarlett, informing him of his son Charles' demise. Jacob saw it first and did not pass the sad message on to his master. The telegram had planted a seed, an evil seed of a plan in his devious mind. Too long had he been the servant, the serf at the beck and call of his rich masters. Here now was a chance to turn the tables. He discussed the matter with Greta and his son. Oh, I know it had been given out that Jacob's son was dead – died from the fever when he was a lad – but this was not true. Thomas got into trouble with the law around the age of fourteen and landed himself in gaol. Jacob managed to hush the matter up, not wanting the stigma of 'criminal' to be laid upon his family name. He put it abroad that the lad had passed away from the fever. After his jail sentence, Thomas joined the army for some time, eventually returning to the area – to live in Ipswich – probably within the last twelve months. It no doubt seemed cruel and ironic to Jacob that he had a healthy, living son with no prospects while his master's boy, who would inherit the Scarlett wealth, was dead. Who came up with the plan of murder I cannot say, but all three – mother, father and son – were in on it. 'You remember, Inspector, I talked about the three M's in crime: motive, method and mistake.'

Barraclough, who had been scribbling down details in his notebook, looked up and nodded.

'Well, the motive was simple enough: the acquisition of wealth and property. The Steerforths wanted more than Fate had apportioned as their lot upon this earth. Many do, of course, but most do not resort to murder in an unscrupulous attempt to achieve this desire. So we come to method – and it was as ingenious as it was cruel. If Thomas Steerforth could be passed off as the dead Charles Scarlett, the bulk of the Scarlett fortune, including this house, would fall to him when the old man died.'

'So why didn't they just bump off old man Scarlett? Why kill the others?'

Darke grinned. 'Because, Inspector Barraclough, "the others" would know Steerforth junior was an impostor. Even the dog,

Charles' own faithful pet before he went to Terai, would most likely react differently to a stranger. Dogs, like elephants, do not forget. It was too great a risk. Ralph, of course, had the advantage of being very young when Charles went away and of course he is blind, so he was not considered a threat. However his father and sister were obstacles that had to be removed. Isn't that so, Jacob?'

The old servant failed to respond. He stared back tight-lipped at his questioner, but his eyes moistened with, Darke surmised, a mixture of suppressed anger and despair.

'Thomas' passing resemblance to Charles could fool the casual observer, but not a close relative.'

'So what you're saying, Mr Darke,' said Barraclough, licking his pencil, 'is that this lot here proceeded to bump off most of the family members in order that Thomas Steerforth could get away with the pretence that he was the Scarlett heir.'

'The brain cogs are running smoothly this evening, Inspector.'

'But why go the lengths of recreating the Griswold Phantom?'

'To muddy the waters. They were fantastic, apparently motive-less crimes, which were designed to prompt investigators to look beyond the family, beyond the rational even. When dealing with the supposed supernatural, one usually dispenses with logic. So young Thomas began the process of recreating the legend of the marsh spectre. He spooked a few villagers, parading around by the mire after dark in his phosphorescent cloak to stir up the old superstitions again.'

'This is all lies and damned supposition.' It was the first time Thomas Steerforth had uttered a word since the handcuffs had been placed upon his wrists out on the marsh. He now spoke in a croaky, demented way, as though he were in some trance and certainly not believing the words he uttered. 'You have no proof and, when this charade is over, I will be obliged, Inspector, if you'll contact my solicitor.'

Barraclough threw him a brief, disdainful glance. 'Ah, but we have proof, eh, Mr Darke?'

Luther nodded. 'As luck would have it, I fell into conversation today with Able Squires. He is a walking, talking history book of the village. It was he, Jacob, who told me about your son being spirited away after he fell foul of the law. Nothing escapes old Abe's eagle eye. He knew of your son's misdemeanours and of his enlistment in the army. More pertinently, he knew of the old hut hidden in the undergrowth on the edge of the mire where Thomas used to go as a lad. It was here that he hid his booty from several burglaries he perpetrated as a youth. Even at fourteen he was prepared to grab property that wasn't his. Thanks to Abe, I found that hut today and it still contained treasures: the props of his monstrous deceit. In the recesses of this now decrepit construction I discovered the Phantom Reaper costume, the scythe and certain items of clothing bearing your name, Thomas.'

'They were stolen, then.'

'Game but desperate. Lame and futile, I am afraid. And so I thought I would play out my little charade this evening to give you a taste of your own medicine.' The smile faded from Darke's face and a hard edge came into his voice as he continued. 'Your father added further credence to the belief that the Phantom had returned by describing the apparition of the Phantom in great detail. As he told me, it "started to walk towards me, very slowly, across the surface of the mire. No living man can do that". Indeed, no living man *can* do that – or did. It was a lie. A monstrous lie. But, by Jove, it convinced the superstitious locals, and in doing so, took away the focus from his family and the motive for any such crimes.

'The fact that Jacob Steerforth was the only man to have claimed to see the Phantom do something that no mortal could do – walk across the mire – was the first major mistake in a catalogue of mistakes which murderers always make. The biggest error was bringing the Phantom into this house to kill John Scarlett. It was obvious that the old man was not going to wander out by the Griswold Mire, now that his dog and his daughter had been butchered there. It was most likely that he even refused to walk his own grounds. He was a frightened man. And so our murderers were forced to bring the Phantom here to carry out his bloody deed, thus clearly and foolishly establishing a pattern and a motive for these deaths – these murders. It now became obvious to me that the only person who could really benefit from the deaths was the eldest son, Charles, who had not been seen for ten years. Even his portrait was missing. It had to disappear, of course. It was clear evidence that the fellow who was to arrive claiming to be Charles was an impostor. Jacob lied to me about the time the portraits of the family were painted. Another mistake. Like many painters, including myself, the fellow who created these portraits dated the canvases on the back. If we search the house I am sure we shall find Charles's portrait hidden away somewhere.'

Barraclough stopped writing and grinned. 'I see it more clearly now. It's as you explained this afternoon. With no one to recognise Charles, this scoundrel here could get away with impersonating him and grab all the inheritance for himself.'

'But what about me?' said Ralph.

'Ah, you were seen as the weakling of the family and could easily be manipulated. Besides, killing you off would perhaps be going too far and certainly raise suspicions,' said Darke.

Barraclough nodded vigorously.

'And Greta was in on all this?' asked Carla, with some surprise, looking at the frail creature who pressed her hands against her face as she sobbed silently.

'She was an accomplice, maybe an unwilling one, but it must not be forgotten that she did not at any time do anything to stop the carnage. Quiet acceptance is no excuse.'

Suddenly, Greta tore her hands away from her face and, rushing towards Darke, she spat in his face. 'You can go to hell!' she screamed, raising her hands, talon-like, before him.

Swiftly, Constable Burrows stepped forward and pulled her back, clasping her arms to her sides.

Wiping the spittle away with a cream handkerchief, Darke gave a sardonic grin. 'Nothing in this investigation appeared as it was. Not even gentle Greta.'

The following morning, Luther Darke and Carla left the Grange to return to London. Shortly before their departure, Carla had sought out Ralph to bid him farewell. She found him in the library, sitting quietly by the window, his pale sightless eyes staring out into the garden.

'You are the master of the Grange now, Ralph,' she said, 'and a wealthy man. Make sure you use your new powers wisely.'

Ralph did not turn to her as he spoke. 'I have learned many lessons – hard lessons – in these last few days. And you have helped to guide my thoughts. I have discovered that in some ways I have been weak. I have been self-pitying and morose. Idolising qualities in others without making any attempt to develop my own. I aim to change all that.' He turned to her, a bleak smile on his lips. 'I aim to do something with my life, something that will not only benefit me but others, too.'

She squeezed his shoulder tenderly.

'And if fate should decree that I find myself in London, I hope you will permit me to visit you.'

'Of course,' she said, almost as a whisper. Bending forward, she kissed the young man on the cheek. 'Of course.'

'Apparently, when the police managed to get statements out of them, it emerged that Greta was the driving force behind the whole plan. Indeed, it was she who first read the telegram concerning Charles' death and decided to keep the news from her master. Both husband and son were her accomplices!' Luther Darke gave a bitter laugh.

'I've told you before, Luther, that you underestimate women. We are such still waters.'

It was a month later, and Darke and Carla were dining at Flagino's. That afternoon, Inspector Edward Thornton had dropped in at Darke's house in Manchester Square to give him the latest news on the Steerforth case.

'However,' continued Darke deliberately ignoring Carla's gauntlet, 'it is the son who will be hanged. It was he who killed the old man and the girl.'

'And the dog,' added Carla, pouring another glass of wine for herself and Luther.

Darke shook his head and leaned over the table in a conspiratorial way. 'Actually, Greta killed the dog. Apparently she hated the creature and wouldn't let anyone else do the deed.'

Carla's response was a wide-eyed stare.

'As you observed, my dear, still waters. And at times too still and too deep for this fellow here.' Luther Darke raised his glass. For a moment he stared at the rich red wine sparkling in the light, and then he took a long drink.

6

THE VAMPIRE
MURDERS INTRIGUE

It was not shame but exhilaration that coursed through his veins as he followed the girl up the ill-lighted rickety staircase that led to her room. Caution, conscience and moral rectitude had been abandoned for the uninhibited delights which he believed lay before him. He did not care how degrading this enterprise would seem to others; he just did not care. He could suppress his base desires for only so long.

The girl struggled with the key to her room. She turned to him with a grin, revealing a row of discoloured teeth. 'It's a bit stiff tonight,' she said with a salacious twinkle, the odour of cheap gin wafting towards him. Basically, she wasn't a bad-looking girl, especially if you disregarded the mixture of grime and cheap, lurid make-up on her face. Underneath, her features were even and regular, almost pretty. Not that it mattered to him. Tonight was not for beauty. She looked in her early thirties, but he doubted if she had yet reached the age of twenty.

She gave the door a shove and it sprang open reluctantly with a jarring creak. 'Come on in then,' she said, winking.

The chamber, illuminated by a solitary candle, was far more sordid than he could have imagined. It stank of sweat and poverty. The bed, its main feature, was covered with grey, stained, wrinkled sheets. It was, he mused, probably still warm from the last customer. This thought excited him all the more.

The girl threw her bonnet and shawl on to a chair and began to slip off her dress. 'Now then, dear, I won't be a moment. D'you fancy a drop o' gin? There's some in that stone jar down by the bed head. Me night medicine.' She chuckled. It was an unnerving sound.

As he bent down for the jar, out of the corner of his eye he caught sight of a shadow sliding over the wall in front of him. With a sudden feeling of fear, his body tensed and almost involuntarily he swung round. He found himself facing the third person in the room. There was an impression of a tall figure, white of features and draped in a long cloak. The stranger's gaunt, ashen face closed swiftly on his and the dark eyes flashed wildly with chilling fervour. Before he knew what was happening, this creature had thrown his jaw wide in a feral snarl: and then with a sudden twist of the head, the assailant bit into his neck. It was a savage, forceful bite. An electric pain shot through his body. Nausea swamped him and immediately he felt consciousness draining away. As the web of darkness ensnared him, he heard the girl laughing, laughing, and laughing…

'Sir Percy Llewellyn, a respected surgeon and father of two. What was he doing in a whore's lodgings in the first place?'

'A naïve question, surely, Edward?'

'But a man of his education, intelligence and public standing…'

Luther Darke smiled and swung his cane so that it disturbed a small pile of autumn leaves, scattering their crisp brown bodies around his feet. 'The sins of the flesh take no note of class or breeding. There are times when all men become "the beast with two backs". Restraint is a skill not given to all.'

Inspector Edward Thornton shook his head. 'I'm sorry, but those whimsical words do not explain why an esteemed member of society would risk everything he possessed for a few fleeting moments of sexual pleasure with a common prostitute in Whitechapel.'

'And then rather inconveniently getting himself killed into the bargain.'

It was the autumn of 1897 and the two men were strolling along the embankment by the River Thames. A faint orange sun struggled vainly to be seen through the thick leaden canopy of a grey October sky, and a cool breeze rustled the remaining leaves in the branches overhead.

'What of the prostitute?' asked Darke after a moment, pulling up the astrakhan collar of his long overcoat as the breeze stiffened.

'Oh, we have her. She got herself arrested for being drunk and disorderly earlier that night – before the murder occurred, in fact. When she sobered up she came out with a tale about some woman offering her a few guineas to use her gaff for the night. We've still got her in the cells, but I reckon she knows nothing about the affair.'

'And yet Sir Percy was lured to these insalubrious lodgings by someone. This someone, this woman, was the bait.'

'You mean she was a mere accomplice. The murderer was someone else?'

Darke nodded grimly. 'Indeed. The woman who "rented" the prostitute's room was merely providing the scene of the crime. It seems most likely then that this was a two-handed affair.'

'What is particularly mysterious is the way in which the fellow met his end.'

Luther Darke allowed himself a little chuckle. 'I knew there had to be something a little more recherché about this case than you have already revealed, Edward. The story so far is fairly mundane – and you do not consult me regarding mundane matters. So how did the fellow die?'

'He was bitten in the neck. The jugular vein was severed and he died by bleeding to death.'

Darke raised his eyebrows in surprise. 'Bitten in the neck? Like one of Dracula's victims, eh? Have you read the Stoker book yet?'

Thornton seemed irritated by the apparent frivolity of the question and shook his head. 'The victim was also injected with strychnine.'

'As an insurance. Strychnine – the speediest of poisons. If the loss of blood didn't do for him, the poison would, eh? Now I am intrigued. The violence and brute force required to bite a man in the neck with sufficient savagery to ensure a fatal wound seems at odds with the use of poison.'

'Exactly,' said Edward Thornton sternly, as he gazed into the middle distance where dark silhouettes of small boats glided on the dark shiny waters of the Thames. 'Why indulge the melodramatic ferocity of the bloodletting when the poison is a simpler and more certain means of murder?'

'"Melodramatic ferocity of bloodletting" – we are back to Dracula again. Now, now, no angry glances, please. I am not being face-tious, my dear Edward. The Stoker book was a sensation last year and it may well be that it has inspired some madman to emulate the vampire's methods. And there must be madness here. To have the power and the fury to bite a fellow human until you sever his jugular vein requires not only a mentality and determination beyond the normal, but also great power. I am certain that I could not bite a man to death, whatever the circumstances.'

Thornton's face darkened with concern. 'Surely you are not suggesting that we are dealing with a supernatural creature – a vampire?'

'Well, the assailant is a vampire of sorts; but the vampire of myth and legend kills to acquire blood as a life-giving force. Here, it seems the motive was murder.'

'Ah, but what was the motive for the murder?'

'Well now you put your finger on the key to the mystery. We need to know more about the dead man. Why should Sir Percy Llewellyn be selected as the victim of this particular gruesome crime? I suggest you arrange for me to interview his wife.'

Maria Llewellyn stood by the window and gazed out over the lawn. She was a tall, self-possessed woman in her mid-forties with an icy demeanour. She had a handsome but careworn face.

'I appreciate that this must be a difficult time for you,' Darke said quietly.

The widow turned sharply as he spoke. 'Difficult? How circumspect you are, Mr Darke. Not only have I lost my husband, but also his death occurred in such circumstances that have cast a blight on his morality and the respectability of our marriage of twenty years. Difficult, certainly.' The eyes sparked fiercely.

'You knew of your husband's previous indiscretions.'

'There were none!' The response was immediate and forceful.

Now it was Darke's turn to bristle. He recognised immediately that Lady Llewellyn was playing a part. One she was used to, but one that was founded upon deception. She was the loyal wife with an impregnable marriage. It may well be that she had even deceived herself that this was the case. However, her response was too swift, too ferocious and too defensive to be natural. What once may have been a successful performance now failed to convince. Darke's statement had been an educated guess, but her reaction had confirmed its veracity. He knew that no gentleman found himself by accident in the grimy, diseased streets of Whitechapel late at night, let alone in a whore's bedroom. The toffs came there for a purpose. Under the cloak of night they came for the women, the easy women, who could be bought for a few coins. Women with whom they could indulge their lustful vices for a few hours before returning to their clean, respectable homes up west or in the shires. Here they would shed their sin as easily as slipping out of their coat, giving no thought to the human misery they had left behind. It wasn't the poor who propagated the foul trade of prostitution, but the affluent.

Darke decided to turn the screws in this charade.

'I have proof,' he avowed firmly. It was a lie, but he knew there was no risk of error.

'How?' Her voice trembled now, and the icy stare began to melt.

'Need we wander into those sordid realms? Suffice it to say that I know your husband was not an innocent abroad in Whitechapel on the night that he was so brutally murdered. All I ask from you is some information regarding his visits to this area.'

'How can you ask me such a question? No gentleman...'

'I never professed to be a gentleman, dear lady, merely a seeker of truth. It is my aim to find the murderers of your husband before they have an opportunity to kill again. There is no shame in your situation. You are not to blame for your husband's ... indiscretions.'

Maria Llewellyn sank to a chair. Her stony façade began to crumble. 'Maybe I am. Maybe if I had been more ... If I had been a better wife.'

'How often did Sir Percy stray?'

She paused and took an intake of breath before replying. 'Every two months.' There were tears in her eyes now. 'He used to tell me that he would be staying overnight at his club, but I knew that was not true. I knew where he was going. And he was aware of that. It was an unspoken thing between us. I used to dread the date coming: the first Thursday of every alternate month. As regular as clockwork.'

'"As regular a clockwork" were her very words.' Darke raised a quizzical brow as he imparted this information to his friend Inspector Thornton in his drab office in Scotland Yard.

'I suppose,' said Sergeant Grey, who was also present, 'men do tend to take their pleasure in this fashion, regular-like. For instance, me and the missus...'

'We both take your point, Grey,' interceded Thornton quickly before they learned more than was necessary concerning the sergeant's domestic arrangements. 'I think the point Mr Darke is making is that whoever killed Llewellyn could have discovered this pattern in his movements, making it easier to plan the murder.'

'It certainly strengthens the case for the crime being premeditated,' observed Darke. 'It suggests that this was not a random killing by some madman influenced by vampire fiction. It is more diabolical. We need to know who wanted Sir Percy Llewellyn dead and why they wanted him to die in such a grotesque fashion. And, more importantly, how long will it be before there is another murder?'

Two nights later, as evening ambushed the great city, another murder was indeed being planned. The killer, gaunt of features and wild of eye, stared into the mirror with malevolence. His lips parted, exposing the vicious pointed teeth. At this shocking sight, he emitted a gurgle of pleasure.

It was approaching midnight when Alistair Coombes left his club in Belgravia. It had been a good night. After a first class meal with some of his chums, he had thrashed old Naughton at billiards, something he'd been wanting to do for months. Coombes had celebrated with a few extra brandies.

'Can I get you a cab, sir?' enquired Welbeck, the club porter, as he helped Coombes on with his coat. 'You seem a might unsteady, if you don't mind me saying so.'

'Yes, I damn well do mind you saying so, Welbeck. Watch your tongue.' He thrust the porter aside. He knew there was hidden meaning in the retainer's words. He knew what the old fool was referring to, damn him. 'I'll get my own cab in due course. Goin' to walk a bit. Get some fresh air.' Snatching his gloves from the porter's limp grasp, Alistair Coombes made what was to be his final exit from his club and staggered down the steps onto the rain-washed pavements.

He made his way up the silent street in a meandering fashion, his emotions vacillating between pleasure at his billiard triumph and irritation at the impertinence of the blasted porter. All that … that unfortunate business was in the past. It should be forgotten now, especially by the likes of insignificant ants like Welbeck. As he paused to steady himself by taking hold of the railings, Coombes became conscious of a hansom cab trotting slowly in the road at his side, the steady clip clop of the horse's hooves echoing in the empty street.

'Want a cab, sir? Looks like rain.' The cabby spoke in a high-pitched cockney whine.

Coombes nodded. Why not, he thought. He'd had enough of walking. He raised his cane in a gesture of acceptance and in a clumsy fashion, he clambered into the cab. In an alcohol-thickened voice he called out his address: 'Sturtley Court Mansions, Hampstead.'

Once he was inside, the cab moved off at a brisk pace. Coombes unbuttoned his coat and flung himself back into his seat. Of course, Welbeck, the porter, was right in one sense; he had to admit it. He was unsteady. Drunk even. And now, in the semi-darkness, he began to feel worse. The cab rocked unevenly, while the shadows seemed to shift and vibrate before him in a kind of surreal fashion and he started to feel sick. He closed his eyes to escape from these disturbing visual sensations. As he did so, he heard someone call his name. It was uttered in an unnatural and muffled manner. It hung in the gloom. But the speaker was close at hand. In an instant Coombes snapped his eyes open to discover that he was not alone in the cab. There was a shadowy presence in the seat opposite him.

'Who the hell are you?' he cried, half in anger and half in panic.

'My name is Retribution,' came the unnatural, gargled response. And then suddenly, with a swift, fluid movement, the figure lunged forward with great force, pinning Coombes back in his seat. The assailant leant close over his victim, the face now clearly visible. His victim emitted a gagging scream as he saw the stranger's open mouth and his fearsome teeth poised to attack him – to savage him.

His scream was drowned by the rattle of the cab and the heavy beat of the horse's hooves on the cobbles.

'It's times like this when I wished I'd taken up another profession – like a grocer or something. They never get called out in the middle of the night to go look at a dead 'un.' Sergeant Grey blew into his hands in a futile attempt to warm them. In his hurry, responding to Inspector Thornton's summons, he had forgotten his gloves.

'I can't see you happily handling carrots and spuds all the day, Sergeant,' observed Thornton without humour.

'Probably not.'

The two were in a police cab on their way to Lion Mews in Belgravia, where Coombes' body had been found by a night constable. While on his beat he had encountered an unattended cab, the horse idly chewing the leaves from a privet hedge, and on investigating, the constable had discovered the mutilated corpse inside.

'According to the report I have received, the wounds to the throat seem similar to the Whitechapel case.'

Grey nodded gravely. 'I thought we hadn't seen the last of that blighter.'

Luther Darke was just finishing his breakfast when his manservant, George, announced that he had a visitor.

'At this time of the day?' said Darke with some surprise, consulting his watch. It was eight o'clock. 'It must be a madman or a debtor.'

'Neither, sir. It's Inspector Thornton, sir.'

'Excellent. No doubt he has news of import. Send him in at once and rustle up some fresh coffee and toast, please.'

Moments later, Edward Thornton was sitting by the fire in Darke's drawing room, drinking a hot cup of café noir.

'That should sweep the sleep from your eyes,' said Darke.

'The sleep has been well and truly swept from my eyes for over four hours now. There has been another killing in the night.'

'A vampire murder?'

Thornton winced at this appellation but nodded in affirmation and then recounted the details, such as he had, of the second attack.

Darke listened with undisguised fascination to Thornton's narrative.

'So everything was the same: the savage wound to the neck, the severed jugular, and the injection of strychnine into the bloodstream?'

'Yes,' said Edward Thornton wearily. 'Or at least, at this juncture I can only assume that strychnine was also used. There hasn't been time for a proper autopsy yet.' The heat of the fire and the warm coffee were reminding his body that it was deprived of sleep. 'The cab was stolen earlier in the evening. A young woman hailed the cabby and asked him to lift her heavy case on to the luggage rack. As he did so, someone came behind him and clamped a rag doused in chloroform to his mouth. He was left unharmed to sleep off the drug in a nearby alley.'

'Reaffirmation, as if we needed it, that there are two people involved in this business; and that these victims are specifically chosen. These are not madmen – random killers – otherwise the cabby would be dead also. He was spared – an innocent pawn in their game.'

Thornton nodded in mute agreement.

'And the victim is Alistair Coombes, you say? I've heard of him. A rich and feckless youth. His antics are always appearing in the society columns. Wasn't he involved in some scandal concerning the death of a woman?'

The policeman gave a wry grin. 'The things you know, Luther. That affair was fairly hushed up. Yes, he got drunk one day and for a bet rode a horse in Regent's Park while he was blindfold. The horse bolted and charged into a group of people, trampling a woman to the ground. Subsequently she died from her injuries. Emilia Slawinski was her name, as I recall. I suppose that in essence it was an accident, a stupid and irresponsible accident. Coombes' family pulled sufficient strings with the appropriate judicial bodies so that the charge was reduced to that of a breach of the peace. I remember the case, because I was in court on another matter the day he was up before the judge. He received a stiff fine – which of course he was well able to pay – and the matter was closed. That was some time in the summer.'

Darke looked thoughtful. 'Anger can burn low and suddenly ignite again. And they do say that revenge is a dish best served cold.'

'What are you saying? That these murders are a form of revenge?'

'It is possible. Was this Emilia Slawinski married?'

Thornton shrugged. 'I don't know.'

'Time for you to find out.'

'Are you suggesting that her husband may be our man?'

'It's an idea, and in solving puzzles, that is all that one possesses at the outset: an idea. It would also be useful to see if there is any connection between Coombes, Sir Percy Llewellyn and this dead woman. If you are able dig up any links at all, they may help us to discover the motive behind these killings and prevent further bloodshed. If you could traipse up that avenue of investigation, I'll do some sleuth hounding of my own. Let's meet up at Simpson's in the Strand for lunch; my treat.'

'I'll see you at twelve-thirty, if I'm still awake,' said the inspector, dragging himself from the chair and the soothing warmth of the fire with some difficulty.

Lunchtime found the two men in a quiet booth at Simpson's restaurant dining on roast beef. Thornton's eyes were now bloodshot with tiredness and he approached his meal in a desultory and listless fashion. At times his knife and fork wandered aimlessly over the food before attempting to retrieve a portion. Darke, on the other hand, ate heartily and was in good spirits after what he considered a fruitful morning's activity. His researches at St Bartholemew's Hospital and in Wimbledon had been very instructive.

Spearing a small roast potato on his fork, he waved it at Thornton in a demonstrative manner. 'Did you know that Sir Percy Llewellyn operated on Emilia Slawinski after her accident? I've been doing some digging at St Bart's. I'm very friendly with the registrar there. In detective work it's good to have friends in high places. I was able to tap into the grapevine, as it were.'

'What did you learn?'

'Mrs Slawinski suffered a ruptured spleen, but Llewellyn failed to diagnose the injury. Apparently he arrived late for the operation and as a result, it would seem, he conducted it in a hurry. Now, my friend, that link is too much of a coincidence.'

'Well,' said the policeman, 'you can forget the idea about the husband being the murderer.'

'Indeed. How can you be so sure?'

'He died a month ago.'

Darke pursed his lips. 'I suppose that does let him off the hook.'

'If it's possible to die of a broken heart, that's how he went. The loss of his wife did for the poor devil.'

'"I love thee with the breath, smiles, tears of all my life! – and if God choose, I shall love thee better after death."' Darke raised his glass. 'To the power of the heart which holds sway over all other organs.' He drained the glass and dabbed his lips with the napkin. 'Were there any offspring?'

'The couple were childless.'

'That is inconvenient. Still, we do have the Llewellyn – Coombes link.'

'But what do we do with it?'

'Ah, my friend, you are starved of sleep. Cobwebs are starting to appear in the corners of your mind, along with the spots of gravy on your chin. Off you go to bed and leave me to pummel my brain over this matter.'

Jonathan Kingsland pulled back the net curtain to see who was ringing his doorbell. He spied a tall man, with strong angular features and piercing brown eyes dressed in a long dark coat with an astrakhan collar. He wore a black felt fedora at a jaunty angle. Instinctively, Kingsland pulled back before he could be detected. He would not answer the door to this stranger – or indeed any stranger. A thin sheen of sweat covered his brow. Perhaps the fear that had been growing inside of him was justified after all. He wasn't just imagining that his life was in danger. He had the note to prove it. Oh, what he would give for a drink, but he had sworn himself off alcohol since …

He took the crumpled piece of paper from his pocket and read the scrawled message again: 'If you value your life, come tonight to 14 Broomfield Terrace, Brixton. At ten o'clock. A friend.'

Luther Darke gave one final pull of the doorbell and waited a short time. There was no response. The hallway remained in darkness. With a sigh of irritation, he turned on his heel. He was severely disappointed that this crucial lead had evaporated. Kingsland had probably gone to earth somewhere, or maybe he had taken not to answering the door to strangers. By now he would be aware that his life was in danger, and would be a very frightened man. Hiding would do the man no good in the long run.

It was late afternoon when Luther Darke's note landed on Inspector Thornton's desk. The detective had snatched a few hours' sleep in one of the cells and then had returned to duty. As usual, Darke's missive was brief and cryptic. 'Put a police watch on Jonathan Kingsland,

27 Ashcroft Road, Wimbledon. He is the next victim. In the mean-time, I shall be taking a trip to the dentist. Luther.'

Thornton threw the note down on his desk with a sigh. Why did Darke always have to be so damned enigmatic?

Several hours later, Luther Darke stepped down from a cab in a smart suburban thoroughfare in Wimbledon. It was his second visit there that day. His first had been a reconnaissance. This time it was different.

He paid his fare, made his way up the pathway of 32 Lowther Road and pressed the brass bell situated above the brass plaque which announced: A. Slawinski, Dentist. There were not many dentists with that name in the city of London. Indeed, as Darke knew, there was only one.

A young woman answered the door. She was dressed in black with a white apron, but from her manner and speech it was quite clear that she was not the maid. She peered out into the gloom at Darke, whose face was only dimly illuminated by the light from the hall.

'I wish to see Mr Slawinski, the dentist.'

'I'm afraid that he has finished surgery for today.' The girl's voice was brusque and strained.

'Nevertheless, I wish to see Mr Alexander Slawinski,' said Luther Darke, crossing the threshold, causing the young woman to step back in surprise.

'I am afraid … Mr Slawinski is not here at present.' The young woman quickly regained her composure.

'Then I will wait.' Darke neatly sidestepped the girl, passed through the inner door and found himself in the main hallway. Instinctively, he took the door on the right and entered a brightly-lit room which was obviously the surgery. It contained an array of dental equipment, including the black chair with the reclining seat. Standing at bench, holding a mortar and pestle, was a tall, dark-haired man of some fifty years. He turned abruptly at Darke's entrance. 'What the devil!' he cried in surprise, dropping the pestle into the sink.

'Mr Slawinski, I presume,' said Darke urbanely, bowing.

'Yes. Who are you and what d'you want…?' His voice was deep and readily betrayed his Polish origins.

'My name is Luther Darke, and I come calling about vampire fangs.'

Slawinski's gaunt features paled. 'I do not understand you.'

Darke flashed him a suave smile. 'Oh, I am sure you do. Let us suppose I am an actor – though not as good an actor as you, Mr Slawinski. I am to appear in a dramatised version of Mr Bram Stoker's wonderful novel *Dracula*. I am to play Count Dracula, a Transylvanian nobleman who is a vampire – a creature of the night who sucks the blood of the living by piercing the jugular vein with razor-sharp canine teeth and then drinking their warm blood. Now, I want to wear a pair of fangs on stage. I wish to be convincing. Can you make me a pair?'

'I am a dentist, sir, not a theatrical prop maker. You would be well advised to seek help elsewhere.'

'Maybe I could borrow yours?'

Slawinski's eyes widened in surprise. His mouth opened but no words came out.

'I think…' said Darke and then said no more. A blinding flash of light obliterated his vision and a fierce pain on the back of his head dulled all his senses. He turned awkwardly as his knees gave way and caught sight of the young woman in the white apron. She was holding a large paperweight in her hand. And then the light faded rapidly and was replaced with an all-pervading darkness as Luther Darke slumped to the floor unconscious.

Jonathan Kingsland slipped on his greatcoat and wrapped a muffler around his face. This was not merely to protect him from the chill night air, but also to hide his features. He was very nervous and still unsure whether to respond to the letter he had received or not. It was signed 'A friend' and yet … however, not knowing would be worse. There had been two deaths so far, and he felt very vulnerable. The connection between the victims intimated to him that he was to be next. If this 'friend' could help… he certainly had no idea where the threat came from. And he could not go to the police without exposing his incompetence. He glanced at the letter again, memorising the address: 14 Broomfield Terrace, Brixton. And then he slipped out of the back entrance, unseen by the two constables who were watching the property at a discreet distance from the front.

Shadows of grey crept into his consciousness. They shifted and shimmered before stabilising and then sharpening. Gradually Luther Darke returned to the world. His head throbbed as though miners were excavating there. As he grew conscious of his surroundings, he discovered that he was slumped in a chair – a dentist's chair – staring up at the ceiling rose. As he attempted to pull himself up into a sitting position, a face came into view. It was Slawinski, who wore a look of worried consternation.

Darke grasped the arms of the chair as he struggled to pull himself upright. As he did so, his head throbbed with more ferocity and his vision faltered. It was worse than the most punishing of hangovers.

'Take it steady,' said Slawinski with genuine concern. 'I really am most sorry about this.'

'Not as sorry as I, sir,' said Darke, the words rolling out thickly from his dry throat. 'Do you not have a brandy or whisky? Some libation to ease the pain.'

Slawinski nodded and disappeared from Darke's restricted vision. Slowly, like a man who has just learned how to move his limbs for the first time, Darke dragged himself out of the chair and stood, somewhat unsteadily, on his two feet. Gingerly he explored the top of his head with his right hand until he felt a small lump and a damp patch. The smear on his fingers told him this was blood. He had been well and truly clubbed.

Suddenly, he found a glass of brandy being thrust in his hand. Without hesitation, he downed it in one long, throat-burning gulp.

'It was your daughter who attempted to cave my skull in, I suppose?' said Darke, handing the empty glass to the dentist, who gazed at him in a penitent and sheepish fashion. He nodded. 'She is an impetuous girl,' he said quietly.

Darke shook his head in disbelief at this understatement. 'You are in serious trouble, Slawinski. If what I suspect is true, you are an accomplice in two murders and possibly three, unless I am too late. Where is Kingsland to be killed?'

His face drained of colour. 'How do you…?'

'Never mind how I know. Just answer the question, and it is possible there will be one less death on your conscience.'

Broomfield Terrace turned out to be a row of derelict houses in the seedier part of Brixton. The apprehension that Jonathan Kingsland had felt about this night's venture increased dramatically as he approached the dark, foreboding edifice that was No. 14. Surely there must be some mistake. The street was silent and deserted. Even the gas lamps were dead. Only a full moon graced this grim location with any kind of illumination. Kingsland stood at the gate and stared at the darkened house, the moon and clouds reflected in its smeary windows. No one was here to meet him. He was sure of that. It has been a fool's errand, he thought. An unpleasant joke played upon him – and played upon him by some form of enemy, certainly not 'a friend'.

He gave a silent curse that he had been careless enough to let his cab depart. He was about to turn on his heel, when he heard a voice – a voice calling his name. Out of the shadows of the porch stepped the slender figure of a young woman. Kingsland could see her face clearly, bathed as it was in the pale creamy light of the moon. From the folds of her cape she produced a small lantern.

'Jonathan,' she cooed, 'I am so glad you came.'

'Who are you?'

'You got my note: a friend.'

'But I don't know you.'

'But I know you and all about you.'

Those words, and the manner in which they were uttered, brought a chill of fear to his heart. What exactly did the girl mean by this simple statement? What kind of poisonous innuendo did it contain?

'What do you want from me?'

'To help you.'

'I am not in need of help.'

'Then why are you here?'

It was a question he could not answer without unlocking the awful secret in his heart.

'You see,' continued the girl, softly, 'I know about Emilia Slawinski.'

The name came upon him as a wound and he gave a gasp of pain.

'I know of your neglect the night she was taken to the operating theatre. You had been drinking, had you not, Jonathan? You administered too much anaesthetic, didn't you, Jonathan? Was it to try and silence her screams?'

Slowly, the girl began to move down the path towards Kingsland, who was transfixed by her gaze and what she was saying. It was as though through the power of her words, he had become petrified. 'Sir Percy Llewellyn failed to diagnose a ruptured spleen. He paid scant attention to his patient. After all, he had business elsewhere that night. Pressing business in Whitechapel. So he left you to keep her quiet. But you went too far, didn't you? While Emilia Slawinkski was bleeding to death from internal wounds, you gave her too much chloroform. Which did she die of first, Jonathan: loss of blood, or excess chloroform?'

Kingsland needed to escape. To escape from these words. To escape from the truth that had haunted his dreams. As he turned to run, he faced a tall figure in a long black cape blocking his path.

'Good evening,' came an eerie gurgling voice. 'Good evening … and goodbye.' The figure came closer, the mouth opened wider and the sharp points of his fangs glinted in the moonlight. Kingsland gave a cry of horror as the stranger spread his cloak and embraced him. The creature's face came close to his and his blood ran cold as he felt the terrible fangs grazing his throat.

Suddenly, like the crack of a whip, a pistol shot rang out. Kingsland's assailant gave a scream of pain and froze momentarily, his grotesque mouth agape. Then with arms flailing, he staggered backward, releasing Kingsland from his terrible embrace. He collapsed to his knees with a moan, a red badge of blood smudging the sleeve of his jacket. The girl ran to his side.

It was like some wild nightmare: dark figures on a moonlit landscape, blood and violence. Kingsland was almost sure he would wake up presently. As the girl sobbed over the wounded man, he turned in his dreamlike state to see two men running towards him down the street: the first, dressed in a long coat with an astrakhan collar and black fedora, was clutching a pistol. The other, white-faced, trailing some distance behind, appeared shaken and distressed.

'I am a good shot. I did not aim to kill you, Doctor Munro,' said Luther Darke. 'It is, I am in no doubt, a flesh wound. You will recover sufficiently to stand on the gallows.' He leant down and tugged at the protruding fangs, which seemed to have slipped down over the wounded man's lips. With little effort they sprang free. Darke held them up for inspection. 'A simple but cruel device, Slawinski,' he observed, addressing his companion. 'Metal fangs, so razor sharp that they can cut through flesh like a knife through butter.'

The dentist did not reply but stared guiltily at the ground.

Darke gave a sigh, and producing a police whistle from his pocket, gave it a hearty blow.

'A mug of tea, sir?' asked Sergeant Grey.

Luther Darke responded with a grimace and a moan.

'You should know by now, Grey, that Mr Darke never partakes of tea,' announced the sergeant's superior.

'Terrible stuff. Erodes the lining of the stomach,' observed Darke lightly.

'See if there's some brandy in the medicine cabinet,' said Inspector Thornton, with a smile.

Grey did as he was told and produced a grimy half-empty bottle, the contents of which he poured into a tin mug and offered to Darke.

'You are very kind, Sergeant,' said Darke with little conviction. He took a sip of the brandy and grimaced again.

It was now two hours since the incident on Broomfield Terrace and the vampire murderer and his two accomplices were in cells at Scotland Yard. The assailant, Dr Charles Munro, had received treatment for his flesh wound. Jonathan Kingsland was also in custody until the whole situation had been explained fully to the satisfaction of Inspector Thornton.

'So,' said Thornton, hiding his annoyance and exasperation as best he could, 'since you were determined to handle the finale of this investigation on your own, Luther, I would now appreciate a detailed explanation of events.'

'It wasn't as though I wished to act secretly or alone, but events developed too quickly for me to contact you. I did tell you to keep a watch on Jonathan Kingsland.'

'Indeed you did, but without an explanation as to why.'

Darke touched his temple. 'Things were still formulating in my head when I wrote that note. The facts of the matter had not fully resolved themselves. I knew I took risks, but I paid for them with a small bump on the head and a major headache.'

'Well, I presume that now the facts and details are clear in your mind, and therefore I would be very much obliged if you would share them with me.'

'With pleasure, but may I suggest we involve Doctor Charles Munro in the process?'

The large iron key grating in the lock of his cell door brought Doctor Charles Munro to consciousness. He blinked as the three men entered, one of whom turned up the gas mantle, bathing his grimy domain with a feeble light. With an effort he pulled himself into a sitting position on his bed, a stab of pain in his shoulder reminding him of his wound. He was tall and thin with a melancholic demeanour. What caught Darke's attention was the infinite sadness in his eyes. It was as though he had absorbed the sorrows of the world.

'What do you want?' he asked, surprised at how faint and hoarse his voice sounded.

'The facts. The truth,' said Thornton, clanging the door shut.

'I'm more than happy to give you both. If one of you gentlemen would kindly pour me a cup of water…'

Sergeant Grey obliged and Munro drank the water down in one gulp.

'I suspect that this fellow here – the one who shot me – knows most of the facts already, but I would like to tell you my story in full. I am Doctor Charles Munro. I work as a junior doctor at Bart's Hospital. Some six months ago I met and fell in love with Julia Slawinski, the daughter of Alexander Slawinski, a dentist in Wimbledon. He is a widower. During my courtship of Julia, I grew very close to the Slawinski family, including Alexander's brother Stefan and his wife Emilia. We spent many happy times together. I grew very close to these good people. Even though I was not yet married to my darling Julia, it was as though as I was a part, an important part, of their lives. Perhaps you cannot appreciate how much that meant to me. I grew up as an orphan and although I made the most of the chances life threw my way – earning a scholarship to the grammar school and then to the medical college – I have always missed being part of a family, having people you can call your own. At last, not only had I found love with the most wonderful girl, but I had found my family. Then tragedy struck.'

Momentarily, Munro turned his head away and heaved a sigh, as though he was attempting to gain strength to continue. When he faced his audience once more, his eyes were moist with tears.

'Tragedy struck,' he repeated. 'Emilia was mown down. No doubt you know of the circumstances. That … that … creature Coombes. I was in the hospital that day when Emilia was admitted but I knew nothing about it until later. Until she was dead. She had a ruptured spleen but Llewellyn – late to the operating theatre – failed to spot it. He had other thoughts on his mind. It was the second Thursday of the month, and he was late for his whoring. He left her in the incapable hands of the anaesthetist, Kingsland, who was not sober. Between them – Llewellyn and Kingsland – they were responsible. Along with Coombes, they killed her. There is a grapevine within a hospital, gentlemen, where one can learn many things, things that would appall you. I learned of these things, of Llewellyn's incompetence and Kingsland's … Men of medicine! Hah! They are butchers. Vampires. They spilled Emilia Slawinski's blood…'

'So you sought revenge?' said Darke softly.

Munro gave a bitter smile. 'If you wish to call it that. Retribution is my label. It was only when Stefan's life faded away, pining for the beloved wife he had lost, that I determined to take action. My wife was of the same mind. Yes, Julia and I were married a month ago. Those fiends had behaved like vampires, draining the blood of the innocent without a shred of guilt, and so they should die the same way.'

Darke nodded. 'And so for this venture, you involved Stefan's brother, Alexander, the dentist, who provided you with the fangs to carry out the task. The strychnine was easily obtained from the hospital dispensary.'

'Indeed, indeed. We worked as a team for our joint retribution – but they are innocent bystanders of the crimes that I have committed. I am the murderer, not them. And I am pleased that I murdered the men I did. They deserved to die. I am only sorry I failed to complete my task and that Kingsland escaped his deserved fate.'

By now Munro's face was wiped clean of emotion. Only tiredness was evident. With a heavy sigh, Munro fell back on the bed and closed his eyes. 'There you have it in a nutshell. I can tell you that I have no regrets … no regrets at all. Now gentlemen, I beg of you, let me sleep. I assure you, I fear no bad dreams.'

'I must admit I have great sympathy for the man.' It was later that night, and Luther Darke was at home in Manchester Square.

Inspector Thornton, invited back for a nightcap, sat by the fire, staring meditatively into the dying embers. 'Surely you do not condone his crimes?'

'Do you know Edward, maybe I do. I know that as an officer of the law, a guardian of our peace and safety, you cannot, but as a private citizen I see a kind of dark justice in what Munro has done.'

Thornton shook his head. 'He is a murderer. However justified his crimes may seem, he is a murderer, and he has transgressed the laws of morality and justice. If we exhibited sympathy for all those individuals who feel ill-used and took the law into their own hands, what sort of society would we end up with? As a humanitarian, I can appreciate the motive but I condemn the action. When it comes down to it, God is our judge and we shall all pay our due penalties on that great day.'

Darke stared into his glass. 'I am afraid that I do not share your faith, nor your patience, but thank Someone, I understand your stance. I hope Munro escapes the gallows and his young, pretty wife is treated leniently.'

Thornton raised his glass. 'On that score, I agree totally and will do all I can to help.'

Darke smiled, raising his glass also. 'You are a good man, Edward. You bring a kind of sober balance to our partnership.'

Instinctively, both men burst into ironic laughter.

In the early hours of the morning, Constable Fielding was carrying out his round of the cells in Scotland Yard. At Cell 23A, bearing the occupant J. Kingsland, Fielding pulled back the metal slot which allowed him a spyhole into the cramped chamber. The sight that met his eyes gave Constable Fielding a severe jolt. He felt his whole body break out in a cold sweat. Through the small aperture, he observed the swinging feet of the cell's inmate. His restricted gaze prevented him from seeing the bloated face with the lolling tongue and vacant, staring eyes of the hanged man as he dangled from the rafters by his own belt.

7

THE ILLUSION OF THE DISAPPEARING MAN

It had to be tonight. He had planned it down to the last detail. There was no reason for a delay and, in fact, in order to survive it was imperative that he act now. He just hoped that his nerves held. Working the scheme out meticulously in an abstract form was one thing, but putting it into action was another. He was entering fresh territory now. He had never killed anyone before.

'I don't understand your fascination with this so-called magician, Merlin the Magnificent, and why you have to drag me off to the theatre to see him.' Carla sat back in the cab and shook her head in mild disapproval.

Luther Darke, who was sitting opposite her, leaned forward and gave her a gentle kiss on the lips. 'Because, my sweet, I know you will be thrilled and fascinated by the fellow. And he is not a magician. He is an illusionist. There is a great difference.'

'And what, pray, is the difference?'

'Well, magic is mysterious and inexplicable. There are suggestions of the supernatural about the concept of 'magic' – the black arts and its accoutrements. An illusionist can easily explain all he does. They're tricks, you see. Innocent bits of business to fool the eyes. The illusionist is in essence doing something quite ordinary, quite practical and workmanlike, but because you don't know what he's doing and how it's done – making a dove appear from out of thin air for instance – you are amazed. But you are only amazed because you are ignorant of the mechanics of the deception. If you did know how it was carried out, you wouldn't think it was very special at all. So you see, it's a far cry from magic; it's more … scientific. When you turn the tap on and water gushes out, you don't say, "Ooh, that's magic," because you know about the plumbing and pipes and so on. But some natives in darkest Africa would think of it as magic. It's the illusionist's job to disguise the inner workings of the illusion.'

'You seem to know a great deal about the practice.'

Darke beamed. 'It's one of my interests. You know how the unusual and inexplicable fascinate me.'

Carla returned his smile. 'Yes, I do.'

The Golder's Green Hippodrome was full that evening, but Luther had managed to secure a box for the two of them. Within minutes of taking their seats, the orchestra struck up with a rousing overture. The first half of the variety show featured fairly mundane run-of-the-mill entertainment: jugglers, a couple of singers who duetted in the most strangulated fashion, a droll comedian in a very loud suit and a troupe of performing dogs. By the interval Carla was decidedly bored, and so Darke whisked her off to the bar, where he plied her with champagne to keep her spirits from flagging. They had just returned to their box when the lights began to dim for the commencement of the second half of the show.

'If you'll excuse me for a moment,' said Darke as Carla settled down in her seat. 'I'll be back shortly.' Before she could respond, he had slipped through the door and was gone. Carla was used to Darke's odd behaviour but this seemed very strange indeed. Why on earth should he choose to disappear at this moment minutes before Merlin the Magnificent was due to make his entrance? He was the reason they had come to the show in the first place. Carla gave a gentle shrug, sat back in her seat and turned her attention to the stage. The small orchestra had just finished wading through the turgid overture heralding the second half of the performance. There was a small ripple of applause and then the curtain rose. To Carla's dismay, the two singers from the first half, a very mature husband and wife duo, reappeared to regale the audience with more of their unattractive warbling. In the first half, Darke had observed that they looked as though they had escaped from some embalming room in a nearby hospital. Carla could not help but agree with him.

After three rather painful renditions of what they referred to as 'popular ballads' – a definition Carla did not recognise – they took their final bow. Carla found herself giving an audible sigh of relief as they wandered into the wings. It was only then that she realised that Luther had not returned. She wouldn't put it past him to have sought refuge in the bar to avoid this tortuous mangling of the supposedly 'popular ballads'.

The master of ceremonies now took to the stage to introduce the top of the bill, the main attraction.

'We are pleased, proud, privileged and puffing out our chests to have secured the services for one week only of one of the greatest illusionists in the known world,' he bellowed with manufactured theatrical pride. 'These will be his only appearances in this country.'

This brought an enthusiastic response from the audience.

'He will baffle you. He will astound you. He will amaze you. And he will confound you.'

More enthusiastic response.

'Ladies and gentlemen, all the way from the mystic East, I give you Merlin the Magnificent!'

There was a dramatic roll of drums and a crash of cymbals as two stagehands manoeuvred an enormous silver ball on to the centre of the stage. Carla, surprised at the non-appearance of her companion, nevertheless leaned forward in her seat in order to get a better view of the proceedings. If Luther was going to miss the performance, she was going to savour all this fellow's illusions.

Now a hush had fallen over the audience as the lights dimmed, the silver ball glimmering ghostlike in the gloom. Suddenly there was a burst of flame and the ball seemed to explode. There was another crash of cymbals and the lights came up. The ball had indeed disappeared and in its place stood a tall, good-looking man with dark skin, dressed in an immaculate evening suit. His handsome face beamed out at the audience beneath a luxurious white silk turban. This was Merlin the Magnificent.

Carla stared intently at this charismatic figure and her mouth opened in an expression of shock and amazement, which quickly transmuted itself into one of great amusement. The figure on the stage, his face caked in dark greasepaint to give it an oriental complexion and sporting a thin moustache, was none other than Luther Darke. So, she thought, that's why he had been so eager for her to accompany him to the theatre that evening. He had wanted her to see him perform his tricks in front of a full house. She had seen him execute some sleight of hand magic business with cards and small objects at various soirées they had attended, but she had no idea that he had been working on anything as dramatic or spectacular as a stage act.

Merlin bowed to the audience in acknowledgement of their enthusiastic applause and as he did so, two birds seemed to fly out from each sleeve of his jacket. They circled his head and with amazing swiftness he snatched them from the air, appeared to squash the creatures in his grasp and then threw them back into the air. What left his hands this time was a brightly coloured parrot which fluttered up into the flies. The audience roared their approval. Already Carla was mesmerised.

The act continued with an array of amazing illusions. At the climax of the performance, two volunteers were enlisted from the audience to help. Merlin was handcuffed and the volunteers checked carefully that they were indeed locked tightly. Then Merlin was placed inside a large canvas bag, which was secured with an iron chain. Further checks were made on the lock by the volunteers before they returned to their seats. The lights were lowered as the stagehands doused the canvas bag in petrol. The smile disappeared from Carla's face. This was dangerous. She knew that Luther gained great satisfaction from taking personal risks but this was perhaps going too far. She wanted to stand up and yell from the box, to tell them to stop but it was too late.

There was absolute silence in the audience as one of the stage attendants lit a torch and applied it to the canvas bag. With a great whoosh, it flared into a bright yellow flame. There were screams from the onlookers, who stared in horror, believing that they were witnessing Merlin's certain demise. Carla bit her knuckles, stifling a cry of anguish. No one, it seemed, could survive that fierce conflagration.

When the flames died away, an awful hush descended over the theatre again. By now Carla was on her feet gazing down at the smouldering remains of the sack, her heart sick with fear and despair.

And then she heard the familiar tones of Luther's throaty laugh. With a cry of elation, Merlin the Magnificent suddenly appeared, caught in the spotlight high up in the flies above the stage. With a cheery wave he swung down on a silver rope to land exactly where the remains of the bag were still smouldering. Carla sank back in her chair, her eyes moistening with relief as her lips formed the silent words, 'You bastard.' The audience were on their feet and the applause was deafening. Merlin took his bows graciously and then waved farewell before stepping backwards into the darkness at the rear of the stage, disappearing from sight altogether.

Carla was exhausted, elated, mystified and completely entranced by the whole experience. She had never seen anything like it before. It truly was magical.

Some ten minutes later, she was backstage searching for Merlin's dressing room. The stage door keeper was less than helpful. 'What d'you want wiv 'im, miss?' asked the old timer grumpily.

'I'm a friend,' she said and then added tartly, 'Well, I was.'

The stage door keeper ignored the comment. 'You'll find him down there, in room six,' he said, waving his arm in a vague direction before returning to his paper and glass of ale.

Carla wandered off, squeezing past the crush of backstage visitors and performers. At last she came upon the dressing room with the large number six painted upon the door. Without knocking, she entered.

Luther Darke was standing by the mirror, stripped to the waist, wiping the dark brown greasepaint from his face.

At first he was nonplussed to see Carla. He had expected her to wait for him in the foyer. However, he soon recovered his equilibrium and his face split into a broad grin. 'My darling…' he said warmly.

'Don't you darling me,' she responded frostily, stepping back from his advance. 'How could you do this to me?'

His features darkened. 'Do what?'

'Trick me in this way. Make believe I was going to see a famous magician and … and it was you all the time. And then you set fire to yourself on stage. You could have killed yourself.'

Darke shook his head vigorously. 'No, no, my sweet, I never was in any danger. You don't think I am so irresponsible that I would put my own life at risk?'

'Yes, I do. I saw you climb into that bag and it being set alight.'

'Illusion. You saw what I wanted you to see. It was a trick.'

Carla looked mystified. 'How?'

'Simple. The sack had a secret opening which allowed me to slip through a trap door in the stage. As I did so, I slipped a rag dummy into my place in the sack. I then made my way under the stage to the wings and thus up into the flies while you and the rest of the audience gazed in wonder and horror as the rag dummy was consumed by flames. So you see, my darling, I was never in any danger.'

Carla slapped Darke's shoulder hard. 'But I didn't know that. I thought that...'

He moved forward, took her in his arms and kissed her.

'I didn't realise that you'd be so concerned. I just wanted to surprise you, that's all. Do you forgive me?'

Carla could not help but smile. 'I suppose so,' she said warmly.

'Good. Well let me make it up to you by treating you to supper. There's quite a pleasant little place called Leonardo's just around the corner from the theatre. Let me get this stuff off my face and take you there.'

Carla discovered that Leonardo's was not just 'a pleasant little place' but was in fact an impressive and expensive Italian restaurant. They were greeted warmly by the head waiter, who obviously knew Luther Darke as a regular customer.

The dining room was very busy, but a table had been reserved for them at the far end by the window. Darke ordered a bottle of claret before settling in his seat. 'I've hardly had a drink all night,' he explained.

'So, are you abandoning your career as a painter for a life upon the stage, Mr Merlin?' asked Carla tartly as she surveyed the menu casually.

Darke chuckled at the thought. 'I think not, my sweet. This is my first and last week as a stage illusionist. I just wanted to see if I could do it. It was a challenge. As you know, I have always been fascinated by the thin line that exists between illusion and reality, by what we think we see and what we really see. It's been very useful in my detective work. I was just putting some of my theories to the test. And now the experiment is over. Of course, I will honour my contract with the theatre but on Saturday night, Merlin the Magnificent will pack away his equipment and his silk turban and like one of his doves, disappear from the scene.'

Their conversation was interrupted by a sudden commotion in the restaurant. A newly arrived customer was shouting angrily at the waiter. He was a short, red-faced man with thick-set features and an arrogant gait. 'Don't contradict me!' he boomed, waving his arms wildly. 'I booked a table two days ago, damn you!' Many diners, disturbed by the noisy outburst, turned to watch this extraordinary demonstration.

The little Italian waiter cowered away from him. 'Apologies, sir. I will arrange a table for you immediately.'

'I should think so,' came the loud, ungracious response.

'Charming fellow,' said Carla.

'I know the chap,' said Darke quietly, leaning forward. 'Well, at least I know his face. It is familiar to me…' He snapped his fingers. 'Ah, yes. It's Charles Stone, the property developer.'

'I've heard of him,' said Carla, wrinkling her nose. 'He doesn't seem a particularly nice individual.'

Darke raised an eyebrow. 'Name me a property developer who is?'

A waiter brought the wine. Darke declared it excellent and downed a full glass before the waiter had time to pour any for Carla. They made their choices from the menu and soon forgot about the obstreperous customer and his manic behaviour for the moment, but towards the end of the meal Charles Stone's strident voice was heard again. This time he appeared to be complaining about his food and demanding to see the manager. The waiter scurried away from his table and Stone rose from the table, scraped his chair noisily on the floor and strode towards the gentlemen's lavatories.

'It must take a lot of energy and self-sufficiency to be as objectionable as that all the time,' observed Darke.

Carla nodded. She was feeling tired and the wine had gone to her head. She glanced at her watch: it was half past eleven. 'Heavens,' she cried, 'I didn't know that it was so late.'

'I'll order coffee and then I'll take you home.'

'Thank you. It has been a long evening, and not one without a surprise or two.'

Darke caught the waiter's eye and requested coffee for two, a large cognac for himself and the bill.

Twenty minutes later, Luther Darke and Carla were retrieving their coats from the foyer. As they did so, Charles Stone barged through in front of them, grabbing his own hat and overcoat before stomping out of the restaurant.

'Manners maketh the man,' observed Darke softly, as he helped Carla with her coat.

Once outside, they both pulled their collars about their faces. The night had turned chilly. A pale crescent moon and a smattering of stars decorated the clear, cloudless sky. Across the city they could hear Big Ben chiming midnight. Then suddenly other sounds intruded upon the night: strident, desperate calls for help, followed by a terrified scream. Glancing up the hill in the direction of the cries, they saw two figures silhouetted against the feeble rays of a gas lamp. They appeared to be grappling with each other in a violent struggle. The figures were just beyond the sphere of light and it was difficult to see clearly, but one of them, a man, was shouting in desperation, 'Help! Murder! For God's sake, help!'

'You wait here,' said Darke, making off up the hill at great speed.

'Certainly not,' snapped Carla, following on his heels.

As they grew nearer, the figures disappeared out of sight around a bend in the road. There followed a loud guttural scream and then silence.

When Darke turned the corner he came upon a body stretched out on the pavement. He knelt down and saw that it was Charles Stone, the obnoxious diner. He was alive and breathing heavily, his face bathed in sweat and grime. He gazed up at Darke, his eyes wild with fear. 'I've been attacked,' he panted hoarsely. 'Did he get away?'

Darke glanced around him. Apart from Carla, there was no one else in view. The street was empty and silent.

Carla knelt beside Darke and helped cradle Stone's head in her hands. 'Are you hurt?' she asked.

'I… I don't think so. Not badly, anyway. Just … shocked … he wanted my wallet. He had a knife. My God, it was awful.'

'Well, you're safe now,' said Carla.

'Thank you.'

'Do you think you can stand up?' Darke took hold of Stone's arm.

'Yes, I think so.' Slowly, they raised the man to his feet. There were no traces of swagger and bounce in Charles Stone's demeanour now: he was shaken and afraid. 'Thank heavens there was someone around. Who knows what would have happened if you hadn't come to my rescue.'

'Where did he go, this fellow?' asked Darke, glancing around the empty thoroughfare. 'Did he slip down this alleyway here?'

'No, no. He ran off up the street, away from you.'

'You seem very sure.'

'Very sure.'

'Perhaps you should see a doctor,' suggested Carla.

'No, no. I'll be fine. I just need a brandy to calm me down. If you two kind people will see me home. I only live less than five minutes' walk away … I don't feel safe enough to go on my own.'

'Of course,' said Carla.

'Thank you, and then I can reward you for your endeavours.'

'Naturally, we'll see you home,' said Darke. 'But no rewards are required.'

Carla nodded.

'Oh, I shall insist,' Stone smiled. 'This way, then.'

While making their way slowly up the hill, Stone introduced himself and explained that he'd just been for a quiet meal at Leonardo's restaurant. At the mention of the phrase 'quiet meal', Darke and Carla exchanged amused glances.

As predicted, in less than five minutes they had arrived at Stone's impressive town house where more surprises were in store for them. The street door was ajar, and light from the hallway spilled out on to the stone pathway.

'I don't understand…' Stone exclaimed as he approached the house. 'I locked the door myself when I came out this evening. It is the servants' night off, you see. My wife has a heavy cold and she retired to bed early. That's why I went to Leonardo's alone.'

'We saw you in there,' Darke admitted.

'Ah, did you,' replied Stone distractedly. He shook his head in bewilderment. 'So why is the door open now…?'

On entering the house it was clear that there had been an intruder. Vases had been knocked over, chairs turned on their sides, and drawers opened and their contents tipped on to the floor.

Stone ran to the bottom of the staircase. 'Marjorie!' he cried out. 'Marjorie!'

There was no reply. With Darke and Carla close behind, he ran up the stairs and into the first bedroom on the landing. The sight that met their eyes stopped all three in their tracks. Lying sprawled across the bed in a blue nightgown was the body of a middle-aged woman. A knife had been plunged deep into her breast and the blood was still seeping on to the bedclothes. Although it seemed likely that she was dead, Darke took hold of her hand and felt for a pulse. There was none, although her flesh was quite warm. It was clear that she had not been dead very long. Stone gave a long moan of anguish and crumpled to the floor, sobbing hysterically.

Carla turned to Darke. 'I saw a telephone downstairs. I'd better ring for the police. You keep an eye on Mr Stone, but don't let him touch anything.'

'Call Edward. Let's have someone we know on the case,' said Darke, extracting a visiting card from his pocket and handing it to her. 'His telephone number is on there. He will most likely be at home in bed, but he won't mind being disturbed…'

Carla gave him a wry smile. 'I wouldn't be too sure about that,' she said as she left the room.

With only a small degree of reluctance, Edward Thornton agreed to come along to investigate the matter. While they waited for his arrival, Carla took Stone away from the murder scene to the drawing room downstairs, where he consumed two large glasses of brandy. The alcohol, along with the shock of discovering his murdered wife, seemed to send him into a kind of trance. He sat in a high-backed armchair, rocking backwards and forwards, staring at the floor and sighing.

Thirty minutes later Inspector Edward Thornton arrived, unshaven and somewhat bleary-eyed. He had Sergeant Grey with him, who had similarly been prised from his bed for the occasion. 'You pick your moments, Luther,' said Thornton, gazing down at the dead woman.

'I thought you'd be interested. I know you've been rather quiet of late. So here I am, presenting you with a nice juicy murder.'

'Tell me all about it.'

Darke took a large swig from his whisky flask and then told Thornton of all that had happened that evening after he and Carla had gone to Leonardo's, including details of Stone's strange behaviour in the Italian restaurant and the murderous assault that had taken place on the hill not far from the property developer's house.

Thornton stroked his chin thoughtfully. 'It's a funny one, all right,' he said, gazing around the bedroom. 'It looks as though the intruder murdered the woman first before ransacking the place, which is not the normal course of events in a burglary. There's no disturbance upstairs, so the chap must have come up here specially to kill her. So it seems that he wasn't just after valuables… and, of course, we won't know if anything valuable has gone until Mr Stone is a little more…' He made a gesture with his hands to suggest stability. 'The lady didn't surprise our man because it's clear that she was murdered where she was found.' Thornton took a sharp intake of breath. 'Maybe murder was the motive, and the burglary bit is a bit of show.'

'A sleight of hand, Edward? Very much in keeping with my line of thinking.'

'What is your precise line of thinking?'

'Nothing definite as yet. I agree that murder – rather than theft – appears to be the motive, but as for the rest … well, I'm afraid the waters are too cloudy at the moment, but something tells me that all is not as it seems.'

'And then there's this mysterious attacker in the street. Are you sure you didn't get a good look at him?'

Darke shook his head. 'I can tell you nothing about him, not even his height. He was too far away and in shadow. Carla will give you the same story.'

'You don't suppose he could be the murderer do you?' asked Grey, stifling a yawn.

Thornton pursed his lips. 'At the beginning of an investigation we have to consider every eventuality. What do you think, Luther? Could he have run up here and murdered Mrs Stone and got away before you arrived?'

'It's possible, I suppose, but unlikely,' Darke said. 'I think she was murdered before the attack. The whole affair seems strange. What would be the motive for murdering Mrs Stone, I wonder? I suppose it's possible that someone has a grudge against Stone and wanted to take some kind of revenge against him. He's certainly not the most charming of men.'

'We'll have to ask him if he has any ideas – but not now. He looks like he's had his brain scrambled. Poor devil. We'd better get him to the Yard for the night so's we can interview him in the morning. Perhaps you'd like to be in on that.'

Darke nodded.

'Very well, come along to my office at eleven tomorrow.'

'I wouldn't miss it for the world.'

Darke and Carla walked slowly back to the hill, in search of a cab. Their minds were awhirl with the evening's events.

'I can't put my finger on it, but there's something I'm not seeing,' said Darke softly, almost to himself.

Carla smiled. 'You're not seeing the fellow with the knife.'

'That's true, but then neither are you. And where did he go? He vanished from view pretty sharpish.'

'Rather like you in the sack before they set it alight. The Disappearing Man.'

'Exactly. Just like an illusion.'

Darke found a cab and escorted Carla home, before returning to his own quarters in Manchester Square. His mind was too active for sleep so, slipping on his smoking jacket and pouring himself a large whisky, he sat before the dying embers of the fire and ran over the events of the evening yet again. There was something unreal, contrived about things, as though he and Carla had participated in some kind of new magic act. At first he blamed his over-active imagination. He admitted that his fascination with mystery and illusion led him to see such affectations in normal life. But he knew that this excuse did not carry weight. He was certain that the incidents he had witnessed that evening were not exactly as they had been portrayed. Something was not real. That was his instinct, and he always trusted his instinct. There was some subterfuge at work, but at present he could not fathom what.

He took himself slowly through all that had happened that night, from the moment Carla had entered his dressing room until Edward had arrived at Stone's house. He used his mind as a third eye, seeing himself along with the other characters in the strange drama. It was a three-dimensional dumb show. As the images paraded before his inner vision, he began to get a tingling sensation on the back of his neck.

'Maybe,' he said slowly, opening his eyes, his lips trembling on the brink of a smile. 'Maybe.'

As he sat back in his chair and took a meditative sip of whisky, his cat Persephone emerged from out of the shadows and leapt into his lap.

'Hello, my dear. Where have you been hiding?' murmured Darke, stroking the cat. The cat purred gently in response. 'It's as though you have been conjured out of thin air,' observed Darke dreamily, the thin smile turning into a grin and brightening his features.

The early morning streets were still very quiet as Luther Darke made his way back to Golders Green, to the spot where Stone had been attacked – attacked by 'the disappearing man', as he now thought of him. He inspected the area carefully for some clue as to the assailant's identity. He walked down the narrow alleyway that ran off at a tangent from the main thoroughfare. Stone had been adamant that his assailant had not gone down there, but Darke investigated anyway. He knew that he could not take anything at face value in this matter. Face value is the shield that helps the illusionist carry out his deception. It was a narrow, featureless avenue – featureless apart from an old wooden box tucked into a large crevice in the wall, some six feet down from the road. Darke found no difficulty in pulling the box out from its hiding place and opening the lid. As he examined the contents of the box, he beamed broadly.

At around ten o'clock, Luther Darke picked Carla up for their appointment with Inspector Thornton at Scotland Yard. As they journeyed in the cab, Carla announced, somewhat breathlessly, 'I've received some information this morning which could be very helpful in solving the murder.'

'And so have I,' grinned Darke, holding up a small suitcase.

'Well then, we need to exchange ideas before we meet Edward.'

'I agree. So give me your news. I am all aquiver with anticipation.'

Carla pursed her lips in mock disapproval at Darke's sarcasm. 'You're not the only one who can play detective, you know,' she said tartly.

'I'm aware of that, my dear. Now tell me what you know… what have you discovered?'

'Well, I just cannot accept that burglary nonsense last night. I believe Mrs Stone was murdered for a reason, and the mess downstairs was meant to make it look like a burglary.'

'That's how I see matters, also.'

'I also believe that Stone is involved in the murder. I'm not sure in what way, and how he managed to carry it out, but I think I have discovered a motive.'

'Go on.'

'I rang a friend of mine this morning, a fellow who works on one of the financial papers in the city. I asked him if he knew anything of the fortunes of Charles Stone. Did he! He knew quite a bit about our grumpy diner. Apparently Stone has been involved in several disastrous deals recently and he is heading for bankruptcy. His cachet in the City is at zero. And what is more, it is rumoured that his relations with his wife, his third by the way, were far from harmonious.'

'Interesting,' said Darke.

'So … if you've got a fat insurance policy on your wife, the wife you don't care for any more, all you have to do is bump her off, collect the cash and save your own financial skin.'

'You would have to be a cold, calculating demon to do that.'

'Well, he is, isn't he? Look at the way he behaved in the restaurant last night…'

'That hardly condemns him as a murderer.'

'No … but you know of his reputation as well.'

Darke nodded. 'Of course. I was just playing Devil's advocate. We are obviously thinking along the same lines. In fact, the motive was one of the missing pieces in my theory, and your idea is credible.'

'Credible! It's more than probable.'

'But is it possible? Remember, our friend Stone was in the restaurant last night, round about the time his wife was murdered, and then we saw him being attacked on the way home. How could he have killed her? She'd been dead less than half an hour at the most when we got there.'

Carla slumped back in her seat with a sigh. 'I don't know how. I … I just know he did it.'

Darke chuckled and placed his hand on hers. 'Of course he did it. And I know how.'

The interview at Scotland Yard with Charles Stone was a fruitless affair. He claimed a certain amnesia concerning the 'terrible events of the previous evening' and could tell them nothing that they did not already know. Somewhat angry and frustrated, Thornton was at a loss as to what to do next when Luther Darke made his dramatic announcement.

'I believe that I can settle this matter once and for all and bring the murderer of Mrs Stone to justice. For this, we must return to Leonardo's restaurant late this afternoon.'

At dusk that day Luther Darke, Carla, Inspector Edward Thornton, Sergeant Grey and Charles Stone gathered in the main dining room of Leonardo's restaurant. The owner was also present, and he looked most unhappy. 'I hope this won't take long Inspector, I am due to open my restaurant in half an hour. I don't want my customers to know the police have been here. That will not be very good for business.'

'I'm hoping that it won't take long either,' said Thornton, uneasy about agreeing to this meeting. Darke had been infuriatingly secretive about it, only assuring him that it would clear up 'this nasty business' once and for all.

'I presume there is a good reason for all of this,' snapped Stone brusquely. The grieving widower of the previous evening had

disappeared altogether and in his place was the rude, irritable cur-
mudgeon Darke and Carla had first encountered in the restaurant
the previous evening.

'This is Mr Darke's idea, and it had better be a good one,'
Thornton observed dryly, throwing his friend a glance.

Luther Darke's eyes twinkled mischievously. 'I don't believe it
will be a waste of anyone's time. I just wanted to demonstrate how
Mr Charles Stone here carried out the murder of his wife.'

'Why you blackguard,' roared Stone, who rushed forward, fists
clenched in readiness to attack Darke.

Sergeant Grey stepped forward to restrain him. 'Let him have
his say, sir.'

'It's outrageous. He's telling lies,' Stone cried, wriggling under
his restraint.

'I'll be the judge of that, Mr Stone,' said Thornton. 'Now, Luther,
can you please get to the point?'

Darke stepped forward and gave a little bow, as though he was
about to give a performance. 'It is no secret that Mr Stone is in
great need of money. Also, it is a fact that there is a very large insurance policy on his wife's life, which will provide him with more
than the necessary funds to salvage his business.'

Stone was about to object again, but Grey's firm hand on his
shoulder stopped him.

'So much for a motive to remove the lady. But what about
the modus operandi? That was, if I may say so, quite ingenious.
Mr Stone dined here in this restaurant last night. He arrived shortly
after Carla and I did, around ten o'clock. We certainly knew he
was here, as did all the other customers, because of his noisy com-
plaints and obstreperous behaviour. He was, by his ostentatious and
dramatic performance, making certain that many people would
remember him, thus establishing his alibi. However, he did disappear for a short time to visit the lavatory. Now gentlemen, if you'd
be kind enough to come with me to the lavatories, I can explain
more easily what happened next.'

'I'm coming, too,' said Carla.

'Of course,' agreed Darke.

Once the group had assembled in the small room, Luther Darke indicated a window at the rear of the dank chamber. 'This is generally kept unlocked and…' – he opened the window wide – '…it would be easy enough for a man to slip out of this aperture. Stone lives less than five minutes' walk away from here, less if you run. I have timed the journey. He need only have been absent from the restaurant for about fifteen minutes at the most, giving him time to go home, murder his wife and create an impression of a burglary before returning, climbing back in through the window. He would hardly be missed. No one times someone's visit to the urinal.' Darke laughed at this final observation, but no one else did.

'One other point which Mr Stone overlooked,' he continued. 'When we arrived at his house last night, the door was ajar and yet there was no sign of a forced entry. Obviously Stone had let himself into his quarters to carry out his plan.'

Stone said nothing, but merely glowered at Darke, his eyes bulging with hatred.

Luther Darke then led the party outside the restaurant. It was now almost dark and the stars were starting to break through the deepening blue of night.

'For the next part of my demonstration, I must disappear for a moment. In the meantime, Carla will take up the story.' So saying, Darke turned on his heel and at some speed raced up the hill, carrying with him his small suitcase. All eyes turned to Carla.

'After Mr Stone had created his alibi in the restaurant, he went one step further to strengthen it and establish his innocence. For this, he required a witness. As luck would have it, he secured two: Luther and myself. When he saw us about to leave the restaurant, he pushed passed us, ensuring that he was out onto the street first. On departing Leonardo's, we saw what we thought was Mr Stone being attacked about halfway up the hill.' Carla pointed up the street, and then placing two fingers in her mouth, she emitted a shrill whistle. As she did so, two figures appeared on the bend of the hill at the exact spot where Stone had been attacked the night before. The figures, just touched by the rays of the gas lamp, appeared to be involved in a ferocious struggle. 'Help, murder!' cried one of them.

'My God, what's happening?' cried Sergeant Grey.

'Come along and we'll show you,' said Carla leading the way.

The group moved quickly up the hill towards the struggling figures. As they drew near, they could see that one of the men was in fact Luther Darke, while the other was not a man at all.

'Meet my assailant,' announced Darke grandly. 'It's a stuffed dummy – a bundle of rags in the rough shape of a man, rather like a children's Guy on bonfire night but very convincing from a distance, eh? In shadow and silhouette from some yards away, this bundle of rags takes on the illusion of being a real man, a real assailant. When Stone had caught our attention with his histrion-ics, he slipped around the bend in the hill and quickly disposed of the dummy in an old box which he had secreted down the alley there. So by the time I arrived on the scene, his assailant had gone: the disappearing man.'

'Thus the alibi was strengthened,' explained Carla. 'The poor man had been attacked on his way home. He could have been murdered. He was a victim, too, just like his wife. Then, at his request, we walked him home, so that we would discover his dead wife's body with him. He was leaving nothing to chance.'

'It's a pack of damned lies,' cried Stone, but there was no convic-tion in the voice.

'It was just your misfortune, Mr Stone,' said Darke, 'that unwit-tingly you involved my services in your nefarious schemes. I am rather adept at illusions myself.'

Stone made a move to run, but Sergeant Grey blocked his way.

'Clap the darbies on him and get him back to the Yard,' said Inspector Thornton.

A tirade of obscenities escaped Stone's lips as Grey handcuffed him.

'A very neat job, Luther,' grinned Thornton, patting his old friend on his back. 'How did you work it out?'

'Strangely, the use of a dummy instead of a real man is a ploy used by Merlin the Magnificent in one of his illusions in his stage act at the theatre down the road. It is a case of devious minds thinking alike.'

'And who is Merlin the Magnificent?' asked Thornton with some puzzlement.

'Let's say that he's a close friend of mine, Edward.'

At these words, both Darke and Carla burst into laughter, much to the confusion of their friend.

ABOUT
THE AUTHOR

David Stuart Davies left teaching to become editor of *Sherlock Magazine* and is generally regarded as an expert on Sherlock Holmes, having written six novels, film books and plays featuring the character. He has given presentations on Holmes at many festivals and conferences as well as on board the *Queen Mary II*. He appeared as toastmaster at the Sherlock Holmes Dinner at Bloody Scotland in 2012 – Scotland's first international crime writing festival. He also created his own detective, wartime private eye Johnny Hawke, who has appeared in six novels. David's latest detective thriller, *Brothers in Blood* (The Mystery Press, 2013), is set in the north of England in the 1980s and introduces Detective Chief Inspector Paul Snow. He has just completed the second in this series, *Innocent Blood*. David is a member of the national committee of the Crime Writers Association, editing their monthly magazine *Red Herrings*. He lives in Huddersfield, West Yorkshire.

Lightning Source UK Ltd.
Milton Keynes UK
UKOW03f0335110114

224368UK00002B/3/P